The Reluctant Heart

Books By Janet Lambert

PENNY PARRISH STORIES
Star Spangled Summer 1941
Dreams of Glory 1942
Glory Be! 1943
Up Goes the Curtain 1946
Practically Perfect 1947
The Reluctant Heart 1950
TIPPY PARRISH STORIES
Miss Tippy 1948
Little Miss Atlas 1949
Miss America 1951
Don't Cry Little Girl 1952
Rainbow After Rain 1953
Welcome Home, Mrs. Jordon
1953
Song in Their Hearts 1956
Here's Marny 1969
JORDON STORIES
Just Jennifer 1945
Friday's Child 1947
Confusion by Cupid 1950
A Dream for Susan 1954
Love Taps Gently 1955
Myself & I 1957
The Stars Hang High 1960
Wedding Bells 1961
A Bright Tomorrow 1965
PARRI MACDONALD STORIES
Introducing Parri 1962
That's My Girl 1964
Stagestruck Parri 1966
My Davy 1968
CANDY KANE STORIES
Candy Kane 1943
Whoa, Matilda 1944
One for the Money 1946

DRIA MEREDITH STORIES
Star Dream 1951
Summer for Seven 1952
High Hurdles 1955
CAMPBELL STORIES
The Precious Days 1957
For Each Other 1959
Forever and Ever 1961
Five's a Crowd 1963
First of All 1966
The Odd Ones 1969
SUGAR BRADLEY STORIES
Sweet as Sugar 1967
Hi, Neighbor 1968
CHRISTIE DRAYTON STORIES
Where the Heart Is 1948
Treasure Trouble 1949
PATTY AND GINGER STORIES
We're Going Steady 1958
Boy Wanted 1959
Spring Fever 1960
Summer Madness 1962
Extra Special 1963
On Her Own 1964
CINDA HOLLISTER STORIES
Cinda 1954
Fly Away Cinda 1956
Big Deal 1958
Triple Trouble 1965
Love to Spare 1967

The Reluctant Heart

By
JANET LAMBERT

Image Cascade Publishing

www.ImageCascade.com

MANUFACTURED IN THE UNITED STATES
OF AMERICA

A hardcover edition of this book was originally published by E. P. Dutton & Co. It is here reprinted by arrangement with Mrs. Jeanne Ann Vanderhoef.

First *Image Cascade Publishing* edition published 2001.
Copyright renewed © 1978 by Jeanne Ann Vanderhoef.

Library of Congress Cataloging in Publication Data
Lambert, Janet, 1895–1973.
    The reluctant heart.

(Juvenile Girls)
Reprint. Originally published: New York: E. P. Dutton, 1950.

ISBN 978-1-930009-31-8

Dear Readers:

Mother always said she wanted her books to be good enough to be found in someone's attic!

After all of these years, I find her stories—not in attics at all—but prominent in fans' bookcases just as mine are. It is so heart-warming to know that through these republications she will go on telling good stories and being there for her "girls," some of whom find no other place to turn.

With a heart full of love and pride–
Janet Lambert's daughter,
Jeanne Ann Vanderhoef

FOR MY OLDER GIRLS

Governors Island, New York,
August 10, 1950.

Dear girls:

I have written you this book because so many of you have requested it.

It was written, as the dedication reads, "for my older girls," for those who have been reading my stories a long time. It's your special book. It's even a sort of letter to you, a long answering of the questions you have so patiently asked. I'm gratefully pleased and happy that you wanted it and have thought of you constantly while the chapters unrolled. I do hope you will like it and that its theme will mean something to you when you have problems of your own to settle. Sometimes, meeting a problem takes a lot of reluctant doing, as Penny discovered, but its accomplishment brings a beautiful satisfaction and a very happy pride.

When I finished writing the book, I was pleased with Penny and hope you will be. But whatever you feel and think, here she is. She's yours to enjoy or criticize, and she comes to you with all my love.

Sincerely,

P.S. I haven't neglected you, my younger girls. I hope you will all enjoy *The Reluctant Heart* and won't find it un-

[5]

eventful and too old. But should you be disappointed, don't despair. You will have a story of your own, next spring. It will be about Dria, who is fourteen and has a horse named Star Dream. Perhaps *Star Dream* might even be a good title for the book. Who knows?

The Reluctant Heart

CHAPTER I

THE noontime countryside was as hot as an electric mangle. A curving lid of sky looked ready to clamp down and sizzle a patient world that lay spread and waiting. Trees stood still, their leaves bunched together for protection; flowers bowed their heads as if praying against destruction, and even grass tried to appear freshly pressed and rolling hills flatter. By their meek neatness, they begged the sky to spare them another ironing. Only one foolish gardener braved the heat and scrambled between rows of vegetables, plopping everything she came to into a basket.

"Oh, come on," she urged, when a carrot half-heartedly protested against leaving its hot but happy home. Then she crouched back on her heels to wipe her dripping face on her bare brown arm. "I'm melting," she grumbled happily, enjoying the little brooks of perspiration that trickled along her back and converged into a river at her spine.

Her arm swiped her face dry and hunched shoulders blotted the rivers into a soppy lake on her white shirt. Her chopped-off blue jeans stuck to her legs so she sat down on the dirt path to roll them even higher. Just sitting there, as quiet and unmoving as the rest of her world, caught her attention and she lifted her head to listen to the silence. Not a cricket chirped, not a bird spoke. "All good little creatures are taking naps," she mused, her brown eyes soft and contented. "They're sleeping, like my two upstairs, and waiting for Josh to come home from New York."

A half-forgotten song floated into her mind and she crossed her knees to hum something about a cottage looking cozy at sundown. Sometimes she remembered words, often she improvised; and her voice had risen on "I think I am in Heaven," when another voice, soft-spoken but decisive, joined in from over by the incinerator.

"Penny Parrish," it called, "you get yourself in the shade before you catch a sunstroke. I mean it now; so you move."

The song was broken, the stillness, too, and the singer stood up to look across a hedge of berry bushes. "I'm Mrs. MacDonald," she reminded with dignity and for at least the hundredth time during her five years of marriage. Then she grinned at a small colored woman who stood with her hands folded over a white starched apron. "Trudy," she said, "I never caught a sunstroke in my life, and you know it. I'm busy, so go away."

"You looked mighty busy." Trudy shaded her eyes and moved a few paces nearer, away from protecting shade. She considered the girl on the other side of the hedge, her flyaway chestnut curls, short rolled up pants, bare brown legs and slim hips, and remarked with feeling, "Child, you don't look old enough."

"I'm rising twenty-six, as Dad always says of horses. I'm a grown-up lady and the mother of two. Here." Penny bent over for her basket. She did it by simply folding over, knees stiff, her body making a double highway to confuse a traveling ant. "Take these in for me," she coaxed, coming up as suddenly as she had gone down. "Tell Minna the carrots aren't very large so she can dump the whole mess in with the pot roast; the cabbage, too."

"Are you plannin' not to mind me?" Trudy reached across

the currant bushes for the basket and regarded its donor with the same loving gaze her eyes had held when her charge had been a baby and refused to settle down in her crib.

"This is *my* day," Penny answered, "my be-kind-to-Penny day. I decided so this morning when I saw Josh off for town. I said to myself, 'If he's foolish enough to go into a hot stupid city, *I'm not*. I'm going to stay right here with my beautiful country home.'" She waved an explanatory hand toward a long stone house that nested in green shrubbery, its double row of windows sheltered by green-and-white striped awnings, its end porch screened and protected by one of the quiet beech trees. "I said. . . ."

"It would be kind of embarrassin' if Mr. Josh said the same thing," Trudy interrupted dryly. "Wouldn't it?"

"Why?" Penny's brown eyes opened wide. "Oh, you mean because someone has to earn a living. Well," she conceded, "you have something there. But it seems to me that Josh could buy a play and produce it without wearing himself to the bone—when he's not much but bones anyway—and doing all the casting and directing, too. Or he could wait till it's cooler. September's always cooler and a month wouldn't matter."

Penny's face was as cloudless as the sky above it, happily unconcerned for the future, be it fair or foul, and Trudy turned away. "Good-by, child," she said. And that flat statement parted the bushes behind her.

"Now what do you mean by that cryptic farewell?" Penny demanded, hopping on one foot and rubbing a scratched leg. "I know you meant something because you always do." She linked her arm through her old nurse's and impeded their progress by reaching across for the basket. "Give," she ordered, when they were walking over a wide back lawn. "Just march yourself straight past the kitchen door to the side porch. We'll sit where it's shady and you can lecture me."

"Child, I wasn't wantin' to lecture you. I just promised your mama and papa that I'd take care of you. They can't do it when they're way off in Germany with our army, so I has to."

"Unhuh." Penny shook her head and pushed open the screen door. "That's not it," she retorted, waiting for Trudy to follow her up the one step, then closing the door noiselessly and setting down her basket. "Josh takes wonderful care of me and you aren't fooling me a bit. I'm doing something wrong; so what is it?"

"You was settin' out in the sun."

"I'm always in the sun. I like it. It makes me feel so alive and clean and . . ." Penny planted her feet wide apart and rubbed her hands down her white shirt . . . "and happy," she ended. "I'm so full of happiness all the time that nothing's big enough to hold it but the sunshine." She drew in a deep breath of sweetly scented air and walked to the edge of the porch where rose bushes mingled with hydrangea along a graveled driveway. "Oh, golly," she said, "days are much too short and nights aren't half long enough to give me all the happiness I have to store up, and the memories." She stood looking out at the quiet lawn where a sandbox and a baby's play pen held scattered toys; and when there was no answer she turned her head.

Trudy sat on a straight chair and was shelling the peas. Pods lay on her white lap and she dropped full green pellets into a glass bowl on a table before her. "Pretty," Penny said, admiring the picture, the bright flowered breakfast cloth on the table, Trudy's bent head that had streaks of gray through its black hair now, her tender work-worn hands that had soothed four little Parrishes and were always ready for the three-year-old Parri and the new baby. She was intent on her work, peas spurted into the bowl like distant bursts of gunfire, and Penny walked back to throw herself on the yellow cushions of a glider. "Trudy," she asked, lying on her stomach, her eyes just looking over the glider arm, "do you suppose I'll *always* be as happy as I am now? Can it last?"

"It should, child, if you knows how to guard happiness." The last of the peas covered the bottom of the bowl and Trudy bent over for another handful. "I reckon you've hit on the very thing I was wanting to talk to you about," she went on, straightening up. "It don't seem that you is exactly guardin' yours."

"Why, Gertrude Johnston!" Penny's eyes rose until her whole surprised face was visible. "Shame on you!" she cried. "I spend every minute of my day holding on to mine."

"Yes'm, you is a little close-fisted." Trudy was unperturbed, but she did turn her head to meet the startled eyes that were staring into hers. "I reckon you've heard the sayin' that the closed hand don't ever receive," she said.

"But my hands aren't closed," Penny denied. "They're simply cupped around my happiness. Isn't that enough?"

"Not to most folks. People is like your brother with his farmin'. Mr. David grows a lot but he keeps on growin' more. He plants and reaps, and plants again."

"And isn't happy." Penny pushed herself higher in the swing, saying with unaccustomed passion, "Can't you see? That's what I'm afraid of. David and I grew up and neither you nor Mums nor Dad ever told us that awful things can happen to us. We just knew that army people never have much money and not to wish for things beyond our means. We were taught to want to amount to something, to enjoy the things we did, and to be thankful for the wonderful, unexpected things that happened to us. Well, David was thankful when Carrol fell in love with him. He was thankful when he didn't go blind at West Point; and after he had fought a war and resigned from the army, he wasn't exactly thankful because Carrol had inherited such a lot of money, but he squared his shoulders and started out to do the best he could with it and to make Gladstone into a paying farm instead of a show place. And then what happened to him?" Penny rolled over on her back and pressed both hands across her eyes. "His little son got polio. *That's* what happened. It's a fine reward!"

"Yes'm, it is." Trudy spoke thoughtfully. "It's a mighty fine reward for them to know God heard their prayers and pulled them through. They's given Davy a lot of courage and he gets around fine now on his braces. Davy's a nice little boy."

"Well, mine won't get it, or anything else," Penny replied fiercely. "I'll guard them—even if it means clamping my fists shut and missing everything else I might pick up. Oh, I know what you're driving at," she said, sitting up straight. "You think I'm unhappy because I'm married to a producer and someone else is going to star in a play that he bought for me. Well, I'm not. I haven't even *looked* at the play. I don't want to go back to the theater because I'm happy here in the country. It's what I chose."

"Seems to me you're protestin' a lot," Trudy returned placidly, "and seems I can remember you tellin' Mr. Josh that you could run this house and act with your hands tied behind you. An' you had a lot of fun goin' in to town together, too," she reminded, "workin' and comin' home together at night. You had several years of actin', even before you was married, way back when you kept us all upset at Fort Knox and on Governors Island, me, an' your mama and papa. First you was wantin' a part, any kind of a part, you didn't care just so you got one. Then after you got it, you worried an' worried about your future till Mr. Josh writes you a play hisself and stars you in it. After that there was no holdin' you and you could have gone to the top of the list."

"I didn't have children then," Penny explained patiently. "Perhaps I'll go back when they're grown."

"Time has a way of not waitin'." Trudy gathered the empty pods into her white apron and stood up. "Perhaps it's a good thing you is an actress," she stopped to remark. "Only an actress could talk herself into bein' such a content whippin' post." Then she picked up her basket, laid a loving hand on Penny's ruffled hair, and opened the door to the dining room.

"Huh," Penny said to the empty porch. "Now how did we get into *that?*"

She sat with her hands on her knees, swinging a little, thinking a lot, until the humor of the situation struck her. "Dear, good Trudy," she mused. "She thinks she's a farmer like David, and has planted a little seed. But she's wrong. I do not choose to harvest it. I'm happy just as I am, being a mother."

Shrieks of laughter floated down from an upper window and she jumped up. "Yoo-hoo," she called, "I'm coming." Flying feet took her through the dining room and into a wide, shallow hall papered with bright red roses.

A stairway started primly up along the wall then changed its mind with delicate whimsy and curved back again above a wide, old-fashioned fireplace. The splash of water mingled with Trudy's voice in an upstairs bathroom and Penny let her scuffers tap the carpeted steps without hurrying. At the top she stepped over a brown and white object that had a lazy panting tongue on one end and a contented thwacking tail on the other. "You're foolish, Dog," she told him. "Why lie up here in the heat when you could be out in that dirty hole you dug yourself?"

Dog had come to the MacDonalds from David's. He was a pointer, son of champion hunters, and meant for Josh. David had sent him over in the station wagon, stylishly equipped with his registration papers, bags of special puppy food, cod liver oil, and a fine whining whistle that was to call him in from roaming the fields. He had looked very noble as Penny lifted him out, and all his hunting ancestors would have been proud of the stance he took when she set him on his feet. Head up, tail straight and stiff, his brown spots nicely spaced over thin, taut ribs. Only one spot seemed to have slipped and covered an eager eye.

"Steadfast of Gladstone," she read from his accompanying paper that was his one-way ticket to Round Tree Farm, which wasn't a farm now, but just a piece of middle-sized property. And she added thoughtfully, "You sound like a Pilgrim. Welcome, Steadfast."

Then Parri had trotted up. Small Parrish MacDonald was a pocket edition of her mother. She had missed the family inheritance of natural curls and was topped by a fine brown mop that clung to her neck and turned both under and out as if undecided which way to go; but her eyes were as soft and smiling as Penny's, her little nose as straight, and her mouth as gladsome. "Hello, Dog," she greeted, bending over to exchange kisses and exposing a round expanse of white ruffled panties.

"His name is Steadfast," Penny prompted. "We might call him Steady for short."

"He's Dog." Parri crumpled up on the grass with a mass of sudden wriggling love on her lap, and explained as carefully to her mother as her mother always explained to her, "His picture is in my book. It says he's Dog. He is."

After that, he was Dog. Sometimes Josh called him Steady, hoping he would absorb something from the name, but his hunting instincts vanished with his title and no one remembered what had become of his whistle. He never went far enough away to need it. He simply blotted out Parri's shadow and Penny said he should be paid a nursemaid's decent salary.

"Well, if you're foolish you're faithful," she praised, bending over to pat him and feeling as if she had closed a protective gate behind her when she went along the hall.

The splashing had ceased. Parri sat on the tiled bathroom floor in a yellow sunsuit, while the baby, naked but for a pair of cotton training pants, admired his pink toes on the bath table.

Parri had given him his name, too. Little Josh, or even Joshie, or "the baby," had done very well for his first few months, since he responded to none of them anyway, until Parri's conversations with him had attracted attention. "Josh, you sit up," she would order, pulling on the front of whatever he wore. "Josh, you take your bottle." It was Josh-you this and Josh-you that until Penny, writing to her mother, shortened the spelling and let him become authentically Joshu. *"It's easier,"* she wrote. *"I don't know how you managed between Dad and David, with their identical names, but whenever I call Josh I get Trudy on the run with blankets flying. Now each of us has a name of his own."*

"I'll take them down where it's cool, Trudy," she offered, experiencing the glad rush of love their round little faces always gave her, the triumphant thought of creation. And she stood straight and tall against the doorframe, as if being measured for a great height that towered among the stars. "These two should show you why I don't want to go back to the stage and play at make-believe," she said, wondering how Trudy could think of Joshu's little shoe as just something to be laced, over and back, over and back, and ending in a secure tucked-in knot. Penny's fingers wanted to caress it, and the fat ankle it encased.

"You're always playin' at make-believe." Trudy was imperturbable as she stood the baby on his sturdy platforms and watched his interest in the unaccustomed weights that, aided by her firm brown hands, gave him a new flat-footed security and the idea of becoming a dancer. "I could tell you what you's thinkin' right this minute."

"What?"

"That no other woman ever brought such fine children into the world and that by givin' 'em to you, God has put a special trust in you. He's sayin' to you right this minute, whisperin' it loud enough so even I can hear, 'Penny, child, I'm givin' you the cream of my crop. Of course, I've been sendin' down children for a good many years—I sent your mama a few, but they was sort of run-of-the-mill goods, and she could think about other things while she was raisin' 'em. But these two!

Ah, you's got to guard 'em like an M.P. with a prison detail. I'm urgin' you to stay right behind 'em with your gun cocked.' "

Penny burst out laughing. "You're too smart," he admitted. "I do think that. Perhaps all young mothers do," she added, thoughtful again. "We can't ever be quite as happy when we're away from home as we used to be, not carefree and not caring what time we get back. We find ourselves watching a speedometer needle and not taking chances crossing a street against the light, or wanting to ride horses over stone walls any more. A sort of protective fear comes to us, Trudy."

"A little sensible fear's all right. But it's like the stock in vegetable soup—it makes a fine base but it ain't all the soup. Here, take your two while I neaten myself up for the evening."

Trudy swung Joshu across a bridge of air and Penny let him sit on her hip in the safe frame of her arm while she pulled Parri up. The happiest hours of her day were beginning, and she said gratefully, "You see, Trudy, I *know* I'm happy. I'm not looking ahead or behind me. I'm not wishing I'd done this or that before I married or could do something else now. I don't want one single thing changed about Josh, either. Some women would like to have one or two things altered in their husbands, but I adore every trait Josh has. He's wonderful. His mother got the cream of the crop, too, you see, for her generation; so I don't have to do like a lot of girls after they're married, pretend that everything's perfect when they're so disappointed they cry inside and keep hoping tomorrow will be better. For me, every day is today."

Penny's eyes were glowing, her lips were still parted in a

smile and her voice had ended on a deep note of pure content. "Yes'm," Trudy said lovingly, "it is. Now run along and enjoy it."

Parri danced along the hall and Dog came to life with puppyish enthusiasm. He passed the slower trio on the turn of the stairs and won the race down with a bounce that sent him sprawling. "Hold it," Penny ordered, when he had re-assembled his extremities that still looked unhinged and were taking off in four directions. "We're making a detour."

Her two little talks with Trudy had disturbed her and she wanted to be with Josh, to have his fine gray eyes tell her she was doing right by keeping their happiness safe in Round Tree Farm; and since it would be at least two hours until she could see him, she turned into the long, cool living room.

"There," she said, putting the baby on the gray carpet to admire his new shoes and leaving Parri to a second washing by Dog before she walked the length of the room. A photo-graph of Josh in a heavy silver frame broke a line of books in the high cases that flanked a window and, although he had protested against being so conspicuously displayed, she had his picture in almost every room in the house. Wherever she went, whatever she did during her day, she was with Josh, and with her family, her mother and father, her brothers and little sister.

"I'm always having to ask somebody something," she had argued plaintively, during the first few weeks of her mar-riage, when the whole family rebelled at meeting themselves. "How can I get advice if none of you is here? If I can't see you? How can I tell you I love you if you don't look at me?" So the Parrishes were everywhere and Josh became accus-tomed to meetng his own grave stare or the dull spectacle of himself in a chef's cap and apron, teaching Parri to ride her tricycle, or with his knobby knees protruding from shorts.

Penny went straight to him now and clasped her hands behind her back. "Hello, handsome," she said, knowing he wasn't handsome at all. Josh's cheeks were too thin, and, as little Tippy Parrish had once remarked, "He had so many bones in his face." His black hair was apt to drop over his forehead when he wrestled with a problem and his tie go crooked. His deep-set eyes had been keen narrow slits until Penny's young nonsense opened them to a wider, gayer world than he had known. He was twelve years older than she and no two lives could have been more different. Josh had been conditioned to life by a careless father whose financial affairs were always much or nothing, and who left his son in a school whenever he wanted to travel. Sometimes the schools were expensive and sometimes they were run by charity. Josh had been tossed back and forth between the worlds of the rich and the poor and discouraged. When he was fifteen he had sat in terrified silence beside his father in a rakish racing car and a few months later had walked the leather from the soles of his shoes hunting a job. All that he now had, the security of his home and the warm, eager love of Penny, he had earned himself.

Now Penny bent toward him and said, "You don't feel that I'm silly to take care of us for you. I know you don't."

One of her delightful characteristics was that her picture family always agreed with her. They approved her plans, bolstered her courage, and were so completely satisfied with her decisions that she was careful never to erase their smiles or destroy their trust in her judgment.

"Thank you, husband," she said, quickly convinced she

was bowling along on the right course, with all lights green and a clear stretch of road ahead. For one surprised second she thought the photograph winked at her and was about to wink back when Parri's piping voice turned her around.

The blue jacketed manuscript of Josh's new play lay on an end table by the divan and Parri's exploring hands had found it. "This is Daddy's," she said importantly, letting one fat finger slide between the typewritten pages. "He said not to touch it, not even Minna when she dusts."

"Then remove yourself from temptation."

Penny stopped and looked down at the play. It had lain in that exact spot for almost a week, and it was a strange place for it to rest. Upstairs was its proper place, in a room that held two desks and two comfortable chairs. Josh worked at one desk and once Penny had worked at the other. She had sat on her straight chair, hunched over like a school girl while she learned lines or answered her fan mail. An old basket of her great-grandmother's had been a brown nest for the heap of letters, and now all it held was a neat stack of receipted bills. Once a month Penny seated herself at the desk and made short work of the bills. The ones she understood she paid; the ones with credits for returns and too many purchases that came out in an odd number of cents and wouldn't add up to her figures, she simply transferred to Josh's desk with a cryptic message that was nothing but a large question mark or a stick drawing of herself shouting "HELP!" Alone in a living room with the misplaced manuscript, she poked a finger at it, much as Parri had done, pushed back from temptation and marshaled her forces outside.

But when she had settled them under a tree, Joshu in his playpen, Parri in the sandbox with Dog on guard, she postponed her own evening bath to take another surreptitious peek. Josh shouldn't have left this thing around to tempt me, she thought resentfully, standing with her hands clasped behind her back. It's like putting a great big box of candy in a child's room. But so far I've stayed on my diet.

She knew the plot of the play. She knew its every scene and change of pace from listening to Josh's first quick reading and his constant talk of it; but she would not read the heroine's part herself. "No sir, I won't," she said aloud. "It can lie here. It can lie here forever." Then she reached out and picked it up. "Drat Trudy," she muttered, and stalked upstairs, the manuscript tucked under her arm.

Penny's firm intention was to put temptation in its proper place, on Josh's desk, and close the door. The little room was over the garage at the far end of the house, and she turned right to her bedroom instead of left just to glance at her clock. Two hands of a Dresden timepiece clung together for a brief embrace at twenty-two minutes after four and she gave a startled gasp. It was almost time for Josh's tires to crunch on the gravel.

The manuscript landed like a square blue patch on her rose counterpane and she pulled off her shirt. It sailed toward a flowered chaise lounge, missed, and dropped on a white wooly rug, along with faded jeans, socks and scuffers that marked a trail to her rose-and-white bathroom. Water gushed, the air was filled with the clean, flower scent of bath salts, splashing, and snatches of song.

But eventually a different Penny emerged from chaos and left a room that bore no visible signs of battle. An electric fan hummed contentedly at peace restored, and she let it blow against the back of her full white dress without disturbing her neat bronze curls while she made sweeping strokes with a lipstick.

She looked no more than twenty when she danced down the stairs, patting the red roses along her way and untroubled about the manuscript that now lay forgotten on the bottom shelf of her night table.

CHAPTER II

IT WAS almost evening and the birds were bursting their little throats with joy over it. Wary crickets sent out short, shrill messages to one another then nimbly hopped for cover. Hills stood up straighter and the grass lined up its green soldiers in massed formation, proud of having won its battle with the sun and finding no dead in its ranks. Penny released Joshu from behind his bars and helped him become a partner in Parri's baking business. They set tins of pies in a row along the edge of the sandbox, and once she leaned over to touch Parri's flushed cheeks. "Let me feel your hand," she ordered, and sighed with relief when the gritty little palm was cool and moist.

Her eyes kept straying down the road, trying to pierce a clump of woodland and a stone wall where the highway passed, and her ears strained for a horn that always tooted at the intersection. And when she saw and heard the familiar green coupé, she dropped the pie she had just bought and raced across the lawn.

"Oh, Josh," she breathed, risking her life by running in front of the car before it had quite stopped and pushing her arms through the door for a sandy hug, "I missed you so. You can't go in tomorrow."

"I can't? Who says so?" Josh pulled on his brake and leaned out to kiss her deeply.

"I do. Wow!" Penny drew back and staggered, her eyes

crossed. "What a kiss!" she cried. "Is that what you practice in the city?"

"It's what I think about but keep like loose change in my pocket. Here." He tossed out a small square package, then followed it.

"Oh, *candy!*" she said happily, shaking it. "How did you know I'm simply dying for some candy?"

"It's vitamins, idiot, for the kids. You ordered them this morning." There wasn't room for the two of them beside the flowering hedge, not if he shut the car door, and he gave her a gentle push. "Did you want some candy?" he asked.

But she promptly shook her head. "I never touch the stuff," she answered, and leaned toward him with mischief in her eyes. "Not even when you leave it around to tempt me—in the form of a play on the living room table."

Josh gave her a long quizzical look, then grinned. The grin laid a pleat in his thin cheeks and a spray of tucks beside his eyes before he became serious again. "You're too smart, angel child," he said, putting his arm around her and making it a tight squeeze past the bushes and the low stone step of the side porch. "I didn't mean to tempt you with the play, really I didn't. I just thought your days might drag."

"*Drag!*" Penny stopped stock-still on the gravel. "Why, I haven't time *enough!*" she began. Then she pulled away and pointed.

Parri was toiling across the grass with Joshu clasped in front of her. He hung like an oversize puppet, his eyes round with concern for himself, and his mouth open and ready to yell should their zig-zag course end in disaster. "Lord save us, she'll break her back," Josh said, grinning again and charging toward them.

THE RELUCTANT HEART

The three fell in a heap with Josh flat on his back and the children bouncing on his chest before Penny decided to move. She liked the picture they made. It was another snapshot for the memory book she kept in her mind, and she stood watching Joshu's new white shoes flail the air while Parri rose and fell in a spanking trot.

Cool evening air had begun to descend. The relief that makes the more fortunate New Yorkers buy country homes for their children was coming in for its evening shift, and she went indoors for two white cotton jackets. She hated to miss a minute of the fun and was ploughing along hooks in a hall closet under the stairs when Minna waddled out of her kitchen.

Fat and Swedish, with a puff of gray hair in a bun, Minna blocked Penny's way like a bulldozer. "You eat in or out?" she asked routinely, knowing the MacDonalds would rather soak their food with raindrops than sit properly in the dining room. In winter, they preferred a low table before an open fire on the living room rug, and in summer they dined in gay confusion in an outside room they had built. It was called "the room" and was a combination kitchen-dining room affair, with a stove and sink set into the brick wall that marked the back of their property, and it had a glass-topped table and white chairs, protected by a green canvas awning.

"Out," Penny answered, also according to form and knowing the table was already set, but carrying on the ritual by adding, "We'll feed the children there first, and you might as well bring Dog's bowl along with their supper. He hasn't been fed, has he?"

"Ya." Minna enjoyed this deviation from the usual and explained with hearty pleasure and a grim look, "John, he weeds down at the far end and finds Dog's bowl in the sink. When he sets it on the floor without so much as asking my leave, Dog cannot wait for politeness."

It sounded complicated but Penny gathered that John, who was the gardener and a handy man of sorts, not too intelligent and very very deaf besides, had detoured from his own business to interfere with Minna's. Dog had eaten early. His dinner was inside him and nothing could be done about it, so she tried to look vexed, too. "Oh, dear," she said, hoping her tone held conviction, "I'll have to speak to him again. He doesn't mean to be such a busybody, and I suppose Dog begged."

"Dog has better manners. Na." Minna would have liked to see old John put in his place, which would be at the end of the line, for she often felt that he ranked a close second to Trudy. There was no possible way to displace Trudy for she was way up at the head with the family, but Minna hoped to move up a notch if John fell back. She might even have a big stick to hold over him. So she complained, "I had to remove his dirty flower pots from the sink in the room."

"You did? Dear me." Penny had a straight view through the dining room of Josh swinging Parri in the swing under a beech tree. "Dear me," she said again helplessly, holding her coats and wanting to run but knowing she had to stay until Minna's normal good humor returned. "I might look for John," she suggested hopefully. "I suppose he's up in his room and I could scold him."

But Minna foiled that means of escape by reporting with triumph, "Na, he is not in his room. His door to the upstairs of the garage, it is locked. He has dressed himself in his silly blue suit and gone to the village again. Every night he goes.

THE RELUCTANT HEART

I am told that he goes to see a young girl—every night. My friends, they tell me."

She gave an outraged sigh that startled Penny into feeling unrequited love breathing down her neck. My soul, she thought, Minna's crazy about the old fellow. She's jealous and complaining because she likes him. Well, what do you know! Now I will have to do something. She felt a new pity for Minna, almost a bond that stretched between her own love for Josh and this late blooming romance; and she said quickly, "I'd better talk with Mr. MacDonald. He'll straighten John out and see that he stays home more, which he really ought to do when you want him to—I mean when we all do—because this is his home and he should enjoy it." Release lay ahead and she took two halting steps toward it before she stopped and gave council. "Minna," she suggested, trying to cover her rising excitement over the news she wanted to relay, "why don't you ask John to go to your church social with you? I'll bet he'd like to."

"Me? With that old fool?" Minna gave another sigh, but an indignant one this time. It even had a query on the end of it that was made by her raised brows and questioning eyes, and it let Penny say:

"Yes. It would be nice if you could. He gets lonesome, living alone. Of course, I know you don't want to bother too much with him, but I think he kind of does things to make you notice him and to help you, like feeding Dog for you, you know. I'm sure he did that because he likes you. Yes, I'm sure of it," she repeated, taking such straight aim that she wondered why her target didn't feel the impact.

"Na." Minna's broad rear swung around and marched away.

It moved with the dignity of a mountain taking a walk and Penny passed it on the run. "Oh, golly," she mumbled, flying across the porch and leaping the step, "I can hardly wait to tell Josh my discovery."

But it was after eight o'clock before she and Josh were alone in the lulling, gently rocking glider. Stars studded a patch of sky between the trees, little night creatures talked softly to one another, and Josh lounged against the pillows at one end of the swing, a leg in, a leg out, his shoe pushing rhythmically against the tiled floor, his arm holding Penny. She usurped a large portion of the cushions because she bounced about so much. Her head was rarely where it belonged, which was against the chest of his yellow T shirt, but was constantly going up and down and interfering with his cigarette. During her recital of Minna's emotional betrayal she had wiggled so much he was forced to protest.

"Listen," he complained, when she pushed both hands against him and leaned back to watch his reaction, "you're pumping me like an accordion. Go a little easy or my chest won't hold out."

"All right." Penny giggled and dropped her head into the comfortable hollow in his curved shoulder. "Sorry," she said, when he brushed her hair from his face. "I wouldn't be disturbing you, would I?"

"Completely." He held her closer and went on, "Furthermore, I can't see one thing in Minna's dull remarks that could make you think she's carrying the torch for John."

"But she *is*. You didn't hear her sigh or see how mad she looked."

"Is being mad a sign?"

"Of course." Her head quivered for another rise and he

managed to wriggle his arm higher and hold it still. "*I* was awfully grouchy," she said. "When I thought you weren't going to fall in love with me I almost drove Carrol and David crazy and I cried on Trudy. I was even sort of mean to Mums and Dad. I wonder what I would have done," she murmured dreamily, "if you hadn't loved me. What *would* I have done?"

"Married one of your childhood sweethearts probably," he answered, amused because it was so like Penny to worry thoroughly and too late. "Perhaps the handsome Lieutenant Colonel What's-his-name."

"Terry Hayes? Not on your life." The whole swing shook with her denial. "We fought too much. It wore me out to be always making up with him. You and I never fight," she said contentedly, and gave him full credit for their domestic bliss. "That's because you have such a marvelous disposition."

"It's because you're the loveliest person in the world."

"Thank you, darling." A hand reached up and patted his chin.

There was quiet in the swing, each lulled by content and restful motion; but when Josh reached down to stub out his cigarette in an ash tray on the floor, she asked, "You weren't ever really jealous of Terry, were you?" And he answered:

"I don't think so. He was such a darned handsome guy that I don't think it ever occurred to me you wouldn't marry him. He just *looked* as if you ought to."

"Why, Josh MacDonald!" This time nothing he could do held her down. Even though he let out a plaintive wheeze, she crossed her arms on his chest and put her face close to his. "You're a hundred times handsomer than he is," she scolded, her brown eyes looking earnestly into his gray ones. "Some of it shows, but most of it's on the inside. You're so handsome inside that you make me dizzy when I look at you on the outside. What more do you want?"

"Well. . . ." Josh stopped to unravel her tangled sentence and to enjoy her soft pressure on his chest, since it was steady, and he said after due consideration of both, "I might like an inch or so of Hayes' long legs and his elegant profile. It might be exciting to have everyone turn and stare at me. Think what a bang I'd get out of passing a bunch of girls."

"And that's something I've been intending to speak to you about," she interrupted. "Lately I've been noticing that happening to you, my good man. Especially since I've been cloistered in the country and only get in to lunch now and then. You may not be Adonis but you do have a way of wearing your battered old felt hat. And you look sort of Britishly baggy—tweedy, if you know what I mean, especially when you smoke a pipe and hold the bowl in your hand. Oh, I've been watching you—and so have the other girls. Dozens of 'em are always smiling and trying to catch your eye."

"That's because I'm a producer. Word has gone out that I'm casting a play and they all want parts."

"Not Neda Thayne. She *has* a part and she's the worst worshiper of all. She positively glows; and she sits with her beautiful legs crossed and swinging till she looks like a stop signal at a railroad crossing."

"My love, you have beautiful legs, too, and a face that puts Neda's to shame. You even have ten years advantage over her. You aren't serious, are you?"

"No." Penny's arms uncrossed and slipped around his neck. Her face dropped down to hide in the cushion, her cheek pressed softly against his chin. "Josh," she asked in a muffled voice, "is Neda going to play the part you bought for me?"

"I don't know, darling. She's willing to leave her show and give it a try if you don't take it. She's the best I can find for it."

"You don't think I should do it, do you?"

"Not if you don't want to, Penny. We've gone all over that." Josh held her close and stroked her hair. "Your contentment is the most important thing," he said, holding back a wishful sigh. "You're a wonderful mother and we have to think of the children first. I like things fine the way they are and I'll find someone else if Neda doesn't work out. She's a good-looking gal but she isn't too long on brains. Can you help me think of anyone else?"

"No." Penny was not to be diverted by his tone. She lay quietly in his arms and only turned her face enough to talk. "Trudy scolded me today," she said. "She doesn't think I'm making enough out of my life, and she doesn't seem to understand how I feel—you know, about Davy, and not being able to have everything I want, so having to choose what I think is best. I loved the stage but I'm happy this way, Josh, I truly am."

"I know you are, sweet."

"And I can't seem to even *think* of going back. I can't make myself want to."

"Then I wouldn't try."

"I should. We could earn twice as much money if I did. I could help you more than I do and not make you carry the whole load."

"Husbands do that for their wives," he answered. "It's what we want to do; we marry for it."

"Then I should have more ambition for myself. I used to have such a lot and it isn't right for me to lose it." Her hand stole up to cup his cheek, and as her fingers gently massaged it, she talked more to herself than to him. "I read a book once," she said dreamily. "It was an old book that Mums had in our library and I think it was called CLIPPED WINGS. It was about an actress who fell in love with a man and married him. He wouldn't let her go back to the stage and she was miserable through the whole book, even though she adored him. They both were miserable. She was a bird, you see, with her wings clipped. But I'm not. I'm free to go if I want to. But I don't want to. Perhaps I should, though. Perhaps I'm a—a coward."

"Oh, Penny, love." Josh felt a tear leave her long lashes and slide gently down to the ribbed neck of his jersey. It was a warm little tear and was followed by a gentle rain of others, until he said in the dry voice that always managed her moods, "You're drowning me."

"I—know it."

"Then let's go back to Minna and John. Our problem was settled over a year ago, darling, when little Davy had polio and we knew Joshu was coming along to join us. We worked out what was best to do; and if it has it's disadvantages, any other way would have as many, or more."

"Then you aren't unhappy about the way I feel?"

"I love you because you always feel the way you do. You wouldn't be Penny if you didn't. You might be Carrol, or Neda, or a dozen other people, and I wouldn't love you. Why, you might not even look like you."

"I wouldn't care."

"I would. I'd miss the way your mouth quirks up and your straight determined little nose. . . ."

"But it isn't straight." Penny's head popped up. "It turns up at the end, you've always said so. You said it was an inquisitive nose."

"Well, it's getting straighter." Josh bent his head and kissed the contested object. "My spine's tired, Mrs. Mac-Donald," he said. "How's yours?"

"I'm not using it," she answered. "I'm using yours. But I could do with a softer pad under my hip."

"Then what do you say we get our money's worth out of our extra-wide box spring with oversized mattress and sheets that cost twice as much as a regular pair?"

"I'd like to but we haven't decided about how I'm to proceed for Minna," Penny answered, comfortable again but leaving him enough room to shift a little. "And I haven't told you that Carrol telephoned this morning and said they're going to be at Gladstone all the rest of this week and most of next while they have some changes made in Davy's braces and David buys more machinery for his precious farm; and that she doesn't seem the least bit worried because she left little Lang at the shore with just a batch of servants. And I had a letter from Mums, too, and she sounds as if she thinks the army will have to struggle on pretty soon without one good officer over there because Dad's wound is kicking up again. My goodness, Josh!" she stopped to cry, "I haven't told you *anything* yet, have I?"

"Apparently not much. Which tale do you plan to begin on?"

"I haven't decided." She laid her arm across him as she

slid down for further comfort, and commanded, "Stick your foot out and rock us again." Then her thoughts scattered like frightened geese at a shot and she tried to sit up in her narrow trench. "Did you hear Joshu cough?" she asked.

"I heard old man Duckwall's motor backfire up the road."

"Oh. Then I think I'll start on Davy," she decided, dropping back, "because Carrol's bringing him over tomorrow. He'll have to play with Parri and that makes me sad."

"Dear Lord, why?"

The swing was swaying again and Josh managed to keep it moving while he found his crumpled package of cigarettes and lighter on the floor, wriggled out a white cylinder and got it going. "Davy's six years old," Penny answered thoughtfully, "and Parri's only three. She won't play anything quiet. Every time he comes, she runs around like she's obsessed—trying to show him everything, and show off. To the berry patch, to the sandbox, to the brook. She can run like a streak and poor little Davy sort of clumps along behind till I'd like to murder her. I tried to explain, in an off-hand way of course, because I don't want her to see that he's different, but I can't calm her down. She gets too excited over having a guest."

"Does Davy mind?"

"I guess not. He clumps along behind her, and Carrol just sits and knits and looks happy."

"Darling idiot, she's glad her child can play at all. It hasn't been much over a year since they thought they were going to lose him. Don't you think that would make you smile over your knitting?"

"I guess so, but I'd be too nervous to knit. Every time I see the poor little thing, I feel so sorry for him I want to cry. I'll plan something for them to do at a table; and now we'll move on to my next subject."

Josh swallowed a yawn and let his mouth widen into an open door that let out a round fat sigh. "Gosh," he said contentedly, "this beats the theatrical business all to smash."

"Why?"

"Because you have such restful problems." He blew out a cloud of smoke, gave the swing a push that was supposed to last it till the end of the evening, and stretched out again. But Penny asked in a small voice:

"You aren't laughing at me, are you?"

"I'm loving you. Remember when we found this house?"

"Umhum, it was snowing."

"I was in snow up to my knees, and I hated the country."

"And said so. You said Carrol and David were silly to buy this place just because it cut into a piece of their land. You didn't even notice *me*, walking around behind you and saying I wanted to own it, sighing because I didn't have a husband to live here with me, and following you in and out of rooms. You didn't even know I was along till we started home. Then you just fastened my coat around my neck, and you said . . ." Her voice dropped to a poor copy of his as she mimicked, " 'Now don't take cold. I spent a lot of good money on a play for you and I can't afford to lose it.' "

"Well," Josh reminded, amused, "I couldn't. Carrol and David had good money tied up in you, too. They could afford to lose a few thousand but I couldn't afford to let them."

"So you married me. Just to help them out, you married me, and bought this house from them, on long *extended* payments, and you even let them furnish it for my wedding present. That was darn big of you."

"Brother, it was," he returned fervently. "With all my money sunk in my first producing venture, with my name signed on enough promissory notes to paper a room, it took courage to step out and buy a house."

"*And* a diamond ring," she prompted, waving her hand before him.

"A diamond ring and two new suits of clothes. Two suits," he repeated. "I'd never bought but one at a time in my life—and I always got that with two pairs of pants."

"Then what happened? I know, but I want you to tell me."

"Then, my love, we made good. You knocked Broadway for a loop and we put in an upstairs fireplace. Ah, man." Josh took a deep draw from his cigarette and Penny murmured thoughtfully into a bright glow that flared:

"I was a partner . . . then."

"Right, partner, you were. I guess that's what made me feel so contented a minute ago. I thought you were kind of cute with your little problems. I was feeling very superior, and I said to myself, 'Funny little child-Penny. Sweet, loving, soft to hold in my arms—in my swing, in my home.' "

"And then, Josh?"

"Then I began to remember. It's half your house, because you helped to earn it. There's a lot of sense under your nonsense; and talent, a brilliant ability that amounts to genius is covered over by a happy simplicity that is like good earth over a seed that could push through and flower. You seem like a cuddly, muddly little thing; but when you were groaning over Davy and I answered you in the right places, I was remembering your first play and the way you stood up to Miltern Wilde when he tried to push you around in *The Robin's Nest*."

"I had to because he thought I was green." Penny laughed but her eyes were solemn with anxiety over Josh's returning the conversation to its original channel. "It was my first part and he thought he could make me stand with my back to the audience. I had to fight him. I knew I was a goner if I didn't."

"So you stole the scene from him. You got the scene and the audience—and got me fired for defending you."

Both lay silent for a moment, remembering that opening night. After long weeks of rehearsal, it was the first time they had liked each other. In fact, it had caused them to break an armed truce. During their try-out of the play in Boston, Josh, who was on leave of absence from the army due to a nervous breakdown, had sneered at Penny for stopping wherever she happened to be when the National Anthem was played. She stopped in the way of scene shifters or stood defiantly in her dressing room door. He had given up a promising career to enlist in the army, to become one of his country's fighting men, and had been assigned the onerous task of directing musicals for soldiers. Troops marched away from his camp, happy after good entertainment, and more came in. He kept them contented, too, until away they went. It was a continuous discontent for him that was aggravated by a stupid, selfishly ambitious lieutenant until he broke under it. Penny had the fortune, bad at the time but ending in good, to come into his life when he was trying to keep his nerves from shooting straight out through his skin. Josh had promptly tagged her as an amateur, the pretty daughter of just another blasted army officer; and it wasn't until she had put a ruthless veteran of the stage in his place—which was with his back to the audience and following her around in a furious jockeying for position and complete frenzy over cues—that he had thought her worth notice. In five minutes he had decided she was destined to become a star and that he was the very fellow to make her one.

"Miltern shouldn't have stood on my foot," she said dreamily. "It hurt. I was going to play the scene in a nice polite way until he did that. It was the way Mr. Goss had directed it, sort of insipid for both of us, and how did I know Miltern was mad about it? He'd been all right in Boston, in fact, he'd been very kind and pleasant. And then, when he gets me in front of a New York audience, when he knows I'm up against the real thing and scared about it, wham! he clamps down on my foot. He wanted to play it his way and he thought I'd be afraid to pull out and move."

"You moved all right."

"So I played it my way. But, was I frightened afterward! In spite of the terrific applause, I thought I'd ruined the whole business and I knew I'd disobeyed orders. There just didn't seem to be anything to do but turn in my suit, and when I had got up enough courage to sneak across to the other side of the stage and let Mr. Goss chop my head off, there you were, thumping scenery and yelling that you'd resign if I got fired."

"So I got it instead." Josh laughed comfortably at the memory. "I was a heel not to tell you that Mr. Goss was Uncle Dad to me, that he was fonder of me than my own father had ever been, and didn't mean it," he said, laying his cheek against her hair. "Probably though, if I had, you wouldn't have felt sorry for me and made me walk you home. You wouldn't have dragged my sad tale about the army out of me or coaxed me to let your father start me out right again. I might never have ended up a sergeant with a nick in my arm and a purple heart."

"And you might never have married me. Would you be sorry, Josh, if you hadn't?"

"Sorry? Child, I wouldn't have become a producer and no pretty heads would turn in my direction. I wouldn't have been a success." There was a long moment of silence in the swing and he smoothed her hair and said with his face close to hers, "Speaking of success—do you know who the girl was who persuaded me to sell the great Mark Slaughter a piece of my first play? She was the sweet little thing I was planning to star. She was," he said into Penny's soft giggle. "I'd been angling for the old boy for weeks and he wouldn't touch my show with a ten foot pole. So what did I do in my desperation? I hooked the Junior Parrishes for quite a hunk of their dough. Then I took my sweet little thing, my shy violet, to lunch with Mr. Slaughter, just to show him what he had missed. And then. . . ."

"I couldn't help it, Josh," Penny said, giggling again. "You looked so worried."

"And there she sat, this girl, wide-eyed and innocent. Slaughter was getting sorrier by the minute that he'd turned me down and was trying to buy a piece while I proudly refused to sell. And up she pipes. Do you know what she said?"

Penny's head shook with silent laughter and he went on, "She said, 'Josh, I think it would be good business to let Mr. Slaughter have a small percent of your play. Yes, I think it might be *very* good.' "

"And did you?" she asked politely.

"Sure, it made me. Who was I in the producing end of the game? Just a little fellow nobody knew. Whenever I think you aren't too bright I remember that day. I saw Slaughter this morning."

To Penny, Mark Slaughter was a person of the past. Josh was as important now as he, so she dismissed him to ask, "Why don't you think I'm bright?"

"Because you're always so happy. Morons are, too."

"Aren't you? Happy, I mean?"

"When I'm with you, yes. When I'm in town I snarl and fight. Why, you even think the plumber's amusing because he always forgets to bring his tools; you get a kick out of stewing over Minna or Davy, or where to set a vase of flowers; you haven't any sense of time and you play the darndest bridge."

"You know something?" Penny said suddenly, actually sitting up this time. "That's it! You live exactly like you play bridge. You pick up your cards and they're all mixed up—mine are, too, but I leave them that way—then you start sorting. Nothing looks like much at first, but after you move them around a bit, they make a nice, neat pattern, *and* you bid a grand slam."

"Do I ever make it?"

"Always. Even when I lay down a hodge-podge dummy."

"Full of aces and trumps."

"And a couple of jokers that got left in from a Canasta game. Now, tell me about Mr. Slaughter."

"Are you coming down again?"

"No." Penny propped up her knees and rested her chin on them. "I think better this way. What did he want?"

"To trade me a piece of his musical for a slice of *One Step to Heaven.*"

"And you told him?"

"I told him no. Was I right?"

"Definitely." Josh had put his hand against the back of her

thin white blouse and she rested against it as she repeated, "But definitely. It hasn't a chance."

"And what makes you think so?" he asked, curious about the sixth sense she used in her decisions. "The critics have given it a whale of a lot of advance ballyhoo and say his script's as good as *South Pacific*. Mark has two of the top men for his music and all the backing he needs."

"But he wants to make a trade with *you*. Hunhuh. If he's as sure as he says he is, he wouldn't put his eggs in two baskets. Besides," she said, "he called me up and asked me to read the thing and talk to you. I wouldn't give him five cents of my grocery money."

"You read it and didn't tell me? Why, you little rat, that's double crossing me."

"I read it and picked out some of the tunes with one finger, much to Parri's delight, because I wanted to find out if we'd see the thing the same way. If we didn't, if you liked it, I'd have been wrong." Penny slewed around and bent to kiss his grin, then climbed across him. "Come on, smart man," she said. "I'm ready to go to bed now."

Josh let her pull him out of the swing; and when she had him upright, she clasped both arms around his waist and looked up. "Are we trying to go somewhere in this conversation?" she asked.

"Nowhere but to bed."

"It all sounds fishy to me. We haven't talked this much about the past or the theater in years. Are you sure you aren't being very clever and leading me back to—back to. . . ."

"No, darling." He took her hand and gently led her through the darkened house, up the familiar carpeted stairs, where her feet were willing to go.

CHAPTER III

THE birds were up early the next morning for another roasting with their feathers on but Penny ran them a close second. The children had their breakfast on the porch; Parri at the table on a cushion and the thick New York telephone directory, Joshu in the high chair that had served David, then Penny and even the two younger Parrishes, Bobby and Tippy. Bobby, now a plebe at West Point and ranked by upper classmen as something lower than an admiral's cat, was being allowed six inches of hard straight chair to perch on and would have been happy to return to such comfort. Penny meditated over him while she automatically scooped cereal from Joshu's chin and shoved it into his mouth. He was on her agenda for the day but at the bottom of the list which ended, *"Visit Bobby and take him a batch of cookies and a cake—if I have time. (?)"* There wouldn't be time, for the week end marketing had to be done and little Davy was coming.

"Minna?" she called, her thoughts hopping from one thing to another as nimbly as the birds. "Have you seen John around?"

"Ya." The kitchen window was quite close to one end of the porch and Minna had only to lift her voice, which she did. "No good he is, running from me like I would beat him over the head with my spoon. Looking so sly."

"Well, he won't look sly when I get through with him," Penny promised; herself looking sly because John was going to have a lesson on how to choose a wife, one that could cook and lived right under his nose. "Have you thought any more about that social?"

"Na."

Silence reigned in the kitchen, and Parri piped up, "I don't *like* Minna."

"Sh."

"She's mean to John and me and Joshu. I could *murder* her for being mean to us."

"Why, Parrish!" Penny gave complete attention to the young person on the telephone directory while Joshu had to wait with his mouth open for a spoon that had gone off the route.

"That's what *you* say," Parri returned virtuously. "You always say, 'I'd like to mur-r-rder him."

"I do not." Josh appeared in the dining room doorway, and she turned to ask, "Do I say that?"

"What?" He stooped to rub his freshly shaven cheek against hers while he rumpled the brown heads on either side of her, and she repeated:

"Do I ever say I'd like to 'murder' anyone, or anything closely resembling it?"

"You say it all the time. Your whole family says it. 'Honestly,' all of you are constantly saying, 'I'd like to murder that dog—cat—me—you—anything.' I'd like to have a dollar for every time I've heard you say, 'I could just murder myself for doing that.' "

Penny flung back her head and laughed. She laughed with such enjoyment that Joshu had to give an outraged yell to bring her attention back to him. "I stand corrected," she said, spooning rapidly. "And I *will* give you a dollar if I ever say it again. As for you, Miss Parrish . . ." Cream of Wheat plastered Joshu's nose as she bent toward her daughter and said, "I'll give you a—*kiss.*"

Parri chuckled at the tickle of Penny's lips under her round little chin but Joshu screamed. He hated breathing cereal, so blew it out in a shower. "Why don't you murder *him?*" Josh suggested mildly, sitting down and unfolding the morning newspaper that Mr. Duckwall's grandson delivered early every morning. "I might even help you. He shatters my nerves."

"And lose a good alarm clock? No thanks." Penny mopped up the cereal with the same thoroughness she used scraping Joshu's chin with the spoon, then gave the baby a piece of toast and turned back to say seriously, "Parri, don't *ever* make that remark about Minna. She wouldn't understand that it's only a joke, and Mummie's not going to say it, ever again. It isn't a kind thing to say."

"All right, and I won't murder Davy. I like Davy. Will he come pretty soon?"

"After you eat your breakfast."

Dog licked Penny's bare ankle, just as a gentle reminder that he was under the table and being neglected but was too polite to beg, so she sent him down a slice of bacon. Quiet and sunshine through the leaves made a happy pattern on the porch. The men of the family, as Josh often called them, were entertained. Josh had his paper propped against his water glass and his eyes followed the print while his fork made automatic round trips and the baby sloppily worked his four new teeth. Penny had time for a breather. She pushed back a curl that had escaped from the red ribbon which tied her hair in a ponytail, tucked her white voile blouse more firmly into her flowered skirt, then settled down to enjoy it. Parri's head, in two tails that stuck straight out from behind her ears, was bent over her plate. She ate dreamily, elbow on the table, her cheek pressed against a morning-clean fist; and Penny, hating to do it, hating to disturb such a delightful reverie, reached out suggestively to touch the offending arm.

" 'Scuse me," Parri said, then promptly forgot and put it back.

You surely do mind well. Penny thought the words but didn't say them for there was no use being a disciplinarian so early in the morning. Not when the birds hopped so close to the foliage around the porch, when the part in Josh's black hair was so white and shining, when such contented grunts came from the high chair; not when it was warm with a lazy warmth that wilted effort. She let her own arm rest on the white cloth and loved them all.

But later, after Josh had gone off in his coupé and she had whisked the baby upstairs for a bath and his mid-morning nap, she heard a horn give a timid squawk at the gate and went flying down the stairs. The Gladstone station wagon pulled up in the driveway and her beautiful sister-in-law looked out.

"I didn't wake him, did I?" she asked, and explained, "That dumb Dog lay right in my way and wouldn't move."

People often spoke of Carrol Parrish as the most beautiful girl they had ever seen. Her hair was so naturally blonde, her skin so clear, her eyes so blue. Every feature of her lovely face was patrician and cameo clear, and was only saved from cold perfection by a winking dimple in one cheek and the fact that she was quite unconcerned for her beauty and even envied the gypsy charm of Penny. She opened the car door and got out, her green chambray dress as immaculate as the morning.

"Where's Davy?" Penny asked anxiously. "Didn't you bring him?"

"He's in the back, hunting his turtle. Davy?" she turned to call, and a round head with bright, sleekly dampened, pressed-flat curls came up.

"I've found him," Davy said. "I'm coming."

Penny wanted to leap off the step and run to the car but Carrol had spoken so carelessly that she stayed where she was. "Should I . . . shouldn't we . . . ?" she began, before an understanding swallow ended her words.

"He'll manage. Where's Parri?"

"She fell in the brook, of course; slipped in the mud with John standing right beside her. It practically scared me to death because I'd asked him to watch her, but she'll be down in a minute." Penny talked with her eyes on the station wagon and listening to the busy little boy within it. It seemed a long time before he made the distance from the back to the front and stood in the door. He looked so much like David had when he was small, that Penny often felt she should shrink to his size and challenge him to a game of *Slap Jack*. There was a bridge of freckles across his straight little nose and his blue eyes had the same sweet seriousness. She tried to keep her gaze on his face and his brown lean body in navy blue shorts, not to glance down at the cumbersome things on his legs, to hide her pity when he grasped the door with his thin little hands and swung himself out.

"Hi, Aunt Penny," he called, lurching for balance. "I

brought Myrtle over, too. He's kinda scared so we'll have to put him in a pan of water. Where's Parri?"

"She's coming." Penny held herself still while he clumped toward her. It was hard to repeat that Parri had fallen into the brook because only a year ago Davy had tumbled around in the shallow water, but she made herself say it. "She had to put on a clean sunsuit," she ended, sitting down on the step and waiting for him.

"She's dumb." Davy put his white box on her lap and offered, "You can look at Myrtle if you want to but don't let him out. Daddy lost him last night and he hid under a radiator." He worked the lid loose for her and added anxiously, "I guess it kinda upset him. There he is. See? He has his name written on him, right there on his back."

"Hello, Myrtle." Penny bent her head and touched a shell that looked empty. "Where's his head?" she asked, staying with her face hidden while she blinked back the tears that Davy's braces always caused.

"He's hiding." Davy heard Parri coming and snatched his box away. "I brought Myrt," he shouted, when she skipped in a one-legged hop across the porch. "Let's go get a pan and put him in it."

"I'll bring one." Penny was halfway up when Carrol pushed her back and sat down beside her.

"They'll find it," she said. "Do you want to leave them with Trudy and go marketing with me?"

"I suppose so." Davy was clinging to the screen door and pulling himself up the step; and under the cover of Parri's delighted racket, she said, "I don't see how you do it. I couldn't leave him alone a minute."

"I can't breathe for him, Penny," Carrol reminded gently.

"Not for the rest of his life. Davy has to grow up and be a man, you know. Next winter, we want to put him in school and David hopes he'll even get into a fight or two. That," she said, smiling, "I can't quite see, but I'd rather he'd fight than be babied by other children."

"And he might not have to wear the braces so terribly much longer. What does the doctor say?"

"That his legs are doing fine." Carrol got up abruptly, and although Penny followed her to the car, she wanted to turn back and leave instructions behind; To urge Trudy to let her upstairs work go and follow the children, to post John on guard, to remind Parri again about the brook and to walk with Davy, not run; but she slid meekly onto the leather seat and Carrol had started her motor before she cried with relief, "Oh, my soul, I've left my purse in the house! I won't be a minute."

This was her chance to marshal her forces, and she rounded them up and warned them while Davy was busy giving his turtle a swim in the sink. "Ooday otnay etlay imhay allfay," she said, in the sign language that had worked successfully when she was a child. But he turned and regarded her gravely.

"I won't fall," he said. "Sometimes I do, but I get up again. Daddy says I have to fall down sometimes, everybody does."

"That's right, Davy, you do," she answered, surprised that he had understood her. "Parri falls, too."

Parri threw herself on the kitchen floor to prove it, and lay with both legs in the air while Penny explained across her, "I just want to be watchful, darling, about both you and Parri. You see, you're my little guest and I'm responsible

[48]

for anything that might happen to you. Parri fell in the brook this morning and I don't want that to happen again."

"I won't let her." He held Myrtle up to dry and fanned the air with him to quicken the process. "Well," he said, "Myrt's had a drink so I'm ready." In true boy fashion he stuffed the dizzy turtle into the pocket of his brief shorts and asked, "What shall we do now?"

"Let's play horse." Parri was up and prancing, and Penny sighed.

There it was again, one of the games Davy couldn't play; and she suggested, "Why not color? Out in the room? I put some crayons and paper out there and I have some scissors if you want them."

"Well. . . ." Davy considered the offer, mulled it over in his mind, then asked, "She can't draw, can she?"

And Penny had to admit, "Not very well."

The horn sounded again in the driveway, longer and louder than it had at the gate, and she turned to Trudy. "What did *we* do?" she asked.

"Child, you did whatever you thought up, yourself." Trudy's tone was flat and Penny made her a bow.

"I thank you," she said, and marched out the door.

Carrol was leaning out of the car and, without waiting for Penny to run around to her own side, she called, "My goodness, what were you doing?"

"I was trying to think up something for the kids to play." Penny plumped herself down and banged the door shut. "I even asked Trudy what we did when we were little and she said, whatever we thought up."

"Wise Trudy. Why do you make such a fuss?" Carrol

circled the station wagon around a clothes line and out the driveway to the country road while Penny blinked and considered the matter.

"Because I'm a fuss-budget, I guess," she answered complacently. "I'd like to be a nice calm person like you but I get twitchety. And that reminds me."

She launched into a complete account of Trudy's warning about happiness and Josh's prolonged reminiscences of the past and her dramatic ability. Carrol had been her friend long before David came into the picture. When Penny was fourteen, she had gone to visit her grandmother and, much to her family's delight and David's annoyance, had bounced home with a lonely little rich girl who was a year older. Carrol had come to spend a month at Fort Arden, shyly, almost reluctantly, for Kansas and an army post were strange, wild places to her. Eastern schools, governesses, and a father who had no time for her had been her world; but through Penny's eager determination, her father had come there to take her home, and a wonderful new life had begun. It had given her four years of happiness before his death, as a dearly loved daughter, then David. They had shared so much, Carrol and Penny. Tears over death, careers, love, the war, little Davy's illness. They knew each other's thoughts before they were spoken; and Carrol, far better than Penny, was accustomed to sorting out the jumble of emotions her friend dumped in her lap, and deciding what should be kept and used and what thrown away.

So she watched the road and listened; and when Penny finally asked, "Do you think Josh and Trudy are cooking up some kind of a campaign?" she shook her head. "No," she answered thoughtfully. "Trudy might be. She knows how ambitious you were and your mother probably has written her that you'll erupt just about the time it's too late. With Josh, it might be subconscious, wishful thinking. He told David he's having a pretty tough time finding the right person for his play."

"Did he say he wanted *me?*"

"No." Carrol shook her head. "David asked him and he said you were doing exactly right." They had reached Landsdale, a small village with a hilly main street, and she swung the car to the curb. "Shall we join the social hour in the A & P?" she asked, "or do Mr. Bellow's Find and Fancy Foods, first?"

But Penny sat forward on the seat and lifted her face for Carrol to see in profile.

"Has my nose gone straight?" she asked.

"Of course not, silly. Why should it?"

"Josh says it has. He always used to kid me because it looked turned up and inquisitive; and now he calls it straight and determined. Is it?"

"It looks just the same to me." Carrol laughed and turned off the ignition. There was no reason to muddle Penny further, so she hung over the back of the seat to reach her market basket, and ordered, "Come on, you're a housewife now."

Penny was not a very good housewife. She thought she was because her house ran in a sprightly fashion, with Trudy rectifying her mistakes and Minna suggesting better balanced menus than she evolved. She was a happy one, as busy as a polthos plant that runs up and down a stick, getting nowhere; and she pushed her cart from bin to bin in the A & P, around and around the shelves, turning back for items she had forgotten and darting out of line at the checker's desk for several things she suddenly remembered. Her list lay at home on the kitchen table and she envied Carrol the neat way she studied her paper, found what she wanted and checked it off.

A lot of Penny's time was lost by talking with people. Old Mrs. Schultz told all about her cataract and had to be guided around; Miss Clements would have Parri in her kindergarten next year and was voluble about it; Mrs. Bandler was a social climber and Penny tried to trundle her cart in another direction.

"Oh, Miss Parrish," she called, bearing down and wanting the actress, not the harried housewife who was scrambling around after rolling cans of peaches she had knocked down in her flight. "I have such a lovely girl coming to stay— Junior League, you know, and the daughter of Roderick Palmer, *the* Roderick Palmer. I do hope you can drop in to tea one afternoon."

"I'd like to." One can rolled straight to the tip of Mrs. Bandler's expensive white shoe and she said, "Just give it a kick, will you? Unfortunately, I'm so busy just now with— with. . . ." She could think of nothing that rushed her so squatted like a quarterback waiting for the ball to be snapped.

But Mrs. Bandler was not so easily defeated. "I've really been planning a studio party for her," she said. "One of those quaint affairs where each guest does something impromptu, you know? I've invited some simply delightful stars out from New York." She named everyone from Mary Martin through the night club entertainers, and ended, "I'd be so happy if you'd do a monologue for us."

"A—a monologue?" Penny clutched her peaches and stood up. "Mrs. Bandler," she said with complete honesty, "I never did a monologue in my life."

"Then perhaps a scene from one of your plays? You're such a wonderful actress," she gushed.

"I *was* an actress." Penny laughed, while she returned her cans to the neat pyramid on the shelf; and she turned to explain, "Josh and I don't go out very much right now. We're working so hard on his new play." They both blinked at the news. Mrs. Bandler with pleasure over the confidence, Penny to know she was working. "That is," she amended, feeling she had no right to share Josh's glory, "he comes home early and I like to be there to talk things over with him." That took care of her afternoons but it left the evening swinging like an open door, and she hastily closed it by adding, "It usually takes us till midnight."

"And are you going to star in the play?" The climbing center of the country set leaned nearer with an eager little twitter in her voice, the hope of information with which to scoop the columnists, but Penny shook her head.

"I'm just Josh's silent advisor," she said. "And now I must catch up with Carrol because she's ready to go over to Mr. Bellow's. I do appreciate your asking me to tea, and I hope you understand why Josh and I can't accept any engagements for a while."

"I do, indeed, my dear." Mrs. Bandler offered a little fluttery gesture as if she might push Penny's cart for her, even though her chauffeur stood at a respectful distance with her own, and did act as escort to the front of the store. "I'll expect some good tickets for opening night," she leaned over to whisper coyly. "Of course, I'll pay for them, but I trust you to see that I have eight or ten in one of the first three rows. We must give our Mr. Parrish a royal ovation."

"We must indeed." Penny smiled but she felt grim. " 'Our

Mr. Parrish!' " she fumed to Carrol, when they were putting their bags of groceries in the car. "Honestly!"

"Why do you care? It was always happening when you were playing," Carrol returned carelessly. "Josh never minded, and after this play opens and you aren't in it, people will begin to forget. Mrs. Bandler may even want him to get up and do the monologue."

"That I should like to see." Penny stalked across the street and was even more absent-minded about her marketing than usual.

She bought carrots when she grew them and a dozen fresh eggs that had come from Gladstone. She came out of her troubled trance enough to telephone home and check on the children; but when Carrol suggested lunching in a candy store that featured mountainous ice cream concoctions, vetoed it with a positive shake of her head and the announcement, "I can't. I have something important to do."

"Meaning I'm not to stay and eat Minna's muffins?"

"Yep. I'm in sort of a hurry."

Carrol wondered what the sudden rush was, but since Penny didn't offer to tell she didn't ask. Time would bring it out. She drove the station wagon along back roads, chatting of inconsequential things, and when Penny broke into her recital of the changes Davy's doctor had suggested in his treatment, she knew. There was no one Penny worried over more than Davy, but she interrupted, "I told Mrs. Bandler a lie. I'm no help to Josh at all."

"Why, Pen, you are."

"I haven't even read his play—not really read it. How could I be any help to him when I don't even know what I'm talking about? I'm a mess."

"Honey, you're always advising Josh. You gave him the right opinion on Slaughter's musical and you told him you thought *One Step to Heaven* is a good play."

"He knew those things. He wouldn't have taken it if he hadn't, and he'd already turned Mark down. I don't see why he ever comes home."

Carrol looked at Penny's flushed woeful face and knew why. "He comes because he loves you," she answered. "If he didn't want a wife he could have married a lawyer or a publicity gal."

"He married an actress. And now, look what he's got!" The station wagon pulled into the driveway and stopped. "I'll just leave the stuff here," she said, jumping out and pulling her paper bags out on the grass. "Will you come back for Davy or shall I bring him home?"

"I'll come." Carrol knew Davy's day would be long if he waited for Penny to remember him, in the mood she was in, so sat watching potatoes spill out.

"There." Penny slammed the car door and mentally dusted her hands of housekeeping. "John can take it in." Then she poked her head through the window and made a face. "Drat Trudy," she muttered. "And Mrs. Bandler, too. Even you."

"Why me?"

"Because you're so darned perfect and never make mistakes. I'll see you when you come back."

"Perhaps."

Carrol knew what was in store for Penny. A metamorphosis was about to take place; a metempsychosis that would be as painful in its way as toothache. She would suffer and weep. Time would have no meaning; heat, hunger, would be but pins stuck in a hypnotic, for she was about to read Josh's play. For as long as it might take, she would be its heroine.

Where all this was to occur, Carrol had no idea. It might be on the side porch with the children staring in worried wonder, or out by the brook like a dog hiding its wounds. But she did hope to be on hand when it was over, to see what emerged. So she made a slow circle around the clothes line and watched Penny dash up the step and fling open the door.

The house was quiet. Not even Joshu jabbered to himself, for he was part of a picnic by the brook, and Penny sped through the downstairs and upward, straight to her room. The manuscript lay where she had left it but was covered by a magazine and her manicure kit. Her hands were stickily moist when she pulled it out, from nervousness more than heat; and clutching it tightly, she flopped down, flat, on her bed.

"Act I," she read, "Living room of the Traymores' house," and didn't know she saw the words. Her eyes raced on while her damp fingers turned pages. Where was the heroine? Why didn't she come on? What senseless play would wait so long . . . ? Ah, there she was, rolling from the wings in her wheel chair. Penny gave one excited wriggle before her shoulders began to sag, her face change from frowning attention to patient sweetness and suffering. Timorously, as Anne in the wheel chair, she began to speak.

Many times during the long hot afternoon she laid the manuscript down and rolled over to sob with despair. She cried for the girl whose husband kept her an invalid because he preferred a bachelor life of his own, and for herself who would never play the girl. They were one, as Carrol had known they would be; and when slats of sunlight through the Venetian blind grew shorter and shorter until they were but one straight strip below the window sill, she gave up a scene that held a secret practice of walking, stolen hours alone with a fine young doctor who knew what was wrong, and went back to the beginning again.

"I've lost the power," she wept then. "I *feel* it, but I couldn't make my audience feel it—not ten cents' worth. I'm not even any good at this."

So she started over. She worried meaning into the lines and tried them a dozen different ways; she even said them as Neda Thayne might, and liked that reading better. She hated Neda Thayne; she hated herself. Anger burned against Josh for producing a play about a fascinating character who hadn't sense enough to know she could get up and manage her life, who refused to acknowledge real love when it came to her—and then did it with a bang. She hated everything but she ploughed doggedly on.

Her dress was a mass of wrinkles, her face tear streaked, and she was anything but the gay Mrs. MacDonald when her door opened and Josh came in.

"Well, fancy this," he said, and sat down on the side of the bed to take her in his arms.

Penny lay against him and sobbed. She sobbed until his tie was spotted and he had a crick in his back, then she scrubbed her face across his white shirt and wailed, "I'm hot. I'm so *darned* hot!"

Josh put her down on the pillow and went into the bathroom. "Here, child," he said, coming back with a damp cloth and sponging her dripping face. "Of course you're hot, shut up in here." He waved the cloth to cool it, folded it and left it across her forehead while he walked over to turn on the electric fan. "You choose the queerest times," he said, in such a dry voice that she gave him a feeble smile. "What made you pick this afternoon?"

"Because I'm a no-good wife." His hands were so gentle as he cooled the cloth again and replaced it and she was so emotionally exhausted that she almost drifted off in a delightful doze. Her own words sounded far away until she caught their meaning. "Listen," she said, pushing her bandage back, "I'm going to reform. I worked on the play."

"So I see."

"And I liked it. I mean, I liked Anne's part even though it tore me to shreds, and I think Neda could do it. She has a certain something Anne should have . . . a sort of—sort of . . . I haven't got it."

Josh bent and kissed her. He saw misery in her eyes. He saw fear too, something new in Penny, and he said quietly, "You have everything, love, but don't worry about it. Every musician finds it hard to play when he's out of practice and feels unsure. That's a natural thing to have happen. But I'm glad you agree with me about Neda, because I signed her up today."

"You—did?"

"We'll start rehearsals in a couple of weeks." He watched her eyes go shut and wondered what their lids concealed. Was it disappointment or relief? Was she glad Neda would take the part, or had she been about to offer her reluctant self in sacrifice? Whatever it was didn't matter now, and he asked, "Could we have Neda out next week end? I'd like to ask Brooks Cameron too, because he'll take the job of stage manager again and there are a lot of things we should discuss."

"Of course we'll have them." Penny opened her eyes again and there was nothing in them, nothing at all. They just looked glad with her lips. "Shall I plan a party or will you want to work?"

"We'll work, I guess." Even with the fan it was stifling and he got up to take off his wilted gabardine coat. "How about a quick shower and change before dinner?" he suggested, and watched Penny snatch off the wash cloth and sit up.

"What time is it?" she demanded, and twisted around to look at the clock. "Oh, ye gods! Where's Davy? Where are the children?" she cried wildly, running her hands through her wet hair. "What happened to the afternoon?"

"It vanished. Davy's safely at home, Carrol tried to wait but couldn't; and our two are having their supper."

"Well, mercy me!" Penny scrambled off the bed and ran to him. "Josh," she begged, getting in his way as he peeled off his shirt and making his neck hotter with her arms around it than it had been with his collar, "let's work to-night. Let's sit at our desks and really rip into the darned old play; lighting, costumes, everything about it, and with lots of arguments."

"Okay," he answered, kissing the top of her head and loving the abandon with which she had come back to him. "But let's do it on the porch where it's cooler."

CHAPTER IV

PENNY gave so much time to Josh's affairs that there were moments when he wished she hadn't decided to become his helpmate. She exploded from the step like a Fourth of July rocket, and except for the hour and a half it took him to drive home, the pattern of his evening matched the pattern of his day. The house ran with amazing precision. Even Dog was given a bath with special soap lest the chatter of his teeth torturing a flea disturb genius at work, and the children ran on such an earnest schedule that Josh, held in town later and later, was glad to have a bowing acquaintance with them in the morning. Unfortunately, it even turned cooler.

"Now, we'll really pitch in," Penny said on Thursday night, leading him into the living room where she had set up a card table, when he wanted to lie in the swing and hold her in his arms. "I worked out a perfectly swell bit of business for Neda and did a sketch or two for one of her costumes. They're under the script. I'll show you."

Josh sat in the easy chair she had ready for him and she leaned against him while she churned through wasted sheets of her monogrammed stationery. When she finally found two drawings that left almost everything to his imagination, he studied them courteously and wished she wouldn't waft the scent of gardenias so fragrantly and so close to him. "Lovely," he said, looking at the pictures but meaning the perfume. "Does she have to wear a shawl?"

"It's a wispy little jacket trimmed with maribou," she corrected. "I couldn't color it so it would look fluffy, but it should be sort of diaphanous and invalidish, the kind of thing her husband would buy her to make her feel sicker."

"Maribou comes loose from itself and floats around," he reminded, hating to but sure she would rather have honesty than false praise. "It's tricky stuff on the stage and distracts an audience." Like you, he thought, reaching up to encircle her waist, just as she moved away.

"I hadn't realized that. Well, make it lace." Penny stopped in the middle of the room and pensively scratched her ear. "And here's my bit of business," she offered shyly. "I'd better give it to you before we go on to other things. It's where Michael tells Anne she can walk and get up and try it. You have her tottering all the way to him, clear over by the fireplace, but I don't think she could. I think they'd do it this way."

She seated herself in a chair, completely unself-conscious, her hands hanging limply over the arms. Brown and sturdy as they were, her hands had a frail look. Her shoulders, too, seemed to narrow, her whole body wasted away and shrank. For a long moment she looked off into space, then her eyes turned to Josh, as Galatea might gaze at Pigmalion, and she whispered, "Michael, perhaps I can. Perhaps . . . for you . . . I can."

Josh sat quite still. He was watching real drama and he knew it. The fragrance and allure of gardenias were gone. Great wonder spread slowly over her frightened, thin little face. "Michael. . . ." The word was only breathed but so perfect was its diction that it reached him clearly. It was a prayer. The helpless Anne looked at him as if praying. Then she worked herself forward on her chair, lips caught between

[61]

her teeth with the effort, and slowly, slowly, painfully pulled herself upright. One foot even moved out for a hesitant step and she groped helplessly for support from the chair back, without moving her gaze. Than she tottered, gave a plaintive frightened cry, and was gathered into a pair of strong sure arms.

Josh had instinctively jumped at her cry. His table with its blue jacketed script and the silly sketches went over like an upside down cake on the floor. He held Penny to him, covering her face with kisses and swinging her around until they looked like an adagio team gone beserk. "You've got it, baby, you've *got* it!" he shouted, when it was safe for them both to stand. "That darned girl has always looked like something out of a melodrama to me, staggering around like our Nell come home with her shame. There'll have to be a few speeches added to really get her going, but the author can make the changes."

He dropped Penny like a rag doll he was tired of and dived for his play. "Right here," he said, flipping the pages. "That's what's been wrong all the time." Then he stopped, set the table upright and laid the manuscript on it. "No good," he said, quiet again. "I forgot. Fritz is rewriting that act."

"Rewriting it? Why? It's *perfect*." Penny came back to normal, too, and with it her joy dropped. "Josh, why?" she asked again, when he didn't answer.

"We're playing Michael up and Anne down," he answered without looking at her. "I haven't said anything about it, but Fritz is doing a rewrite job. It had to be, honey, and I was going to show it to you when it's finished."

"Oh, Josh." Fortunately the faithful chair was behind her

and she sank into it. "You're going to ruin the play," she said.

"I don't think so. It will be a better vehicle for a team. Jervis Travers is a good leading man and they'll be co-billed."

"What does Neda have to say about it?"

"It's okay with her—she's never been a star anyway, and she knew it when she took the part."

"Oh." Penny sat for some minutes in silence. She watched Josh thumb through the sides of his play, seemingly intent and not wanting to look at her, and she said suddenly, "It's sort of like this chair I'm sitting in, isn't it?"

"What?" He turned around and his grin spread. "I never heard of a play being compared to a yellow chair before."

"I didn't have enough imported silk for the whole thing so I had to do the back in matching velvet. The salesman said lots of channel backs are done that way." She got up and gave the chair a thorough inspection. "I've never been quite satisfied," she said. "I don't like it much, do you?"

"For a chair, it's okay."

"But for a play?"

"Silly one." Josh picked up the rest of his papers and sat down in his directorial seat again. "Now, about these sketches," he began, just as Penny crawled onto his lap.

"I love you," she said. "Oh, dear man, how I love you." She held his bony forehead between her two hands and tenderly massaged his scalp. "If your hair falls out or turns prematurely gray I'll never forgive myself. Every new wrinkle you get is carved in my heart. I feel—awful!"

"You smell good." He sniffed appreciatively into her pink lace and she let her hands slide down to his cheeks.

"Darling," she whispered softly, just as a long piercing scream came from above.

[63]

"Daddy — Mummie — Mummie — *Mummie!*" Parrish screamed. And Penny and Josh jumped up and raced each other through the hall and up the stairway.

"We're coming, baby," Penny called. "We're right here, we're coming."

Dog lay in his usual place at the top and, rising courteously, blocked their way. They scrambled around him and Penny was first to reach the switch that controlled a lamp. Parri sat up in her bed. Her hair was hot and damp; her round little face on its stem of neck stuck out of a cotton snuggle bunny that had come up with her and made a tent, and her eyes were wide with terror.

"We're here, baby," Josh soothed, while Penny untied tapes so he could lift her out. "Tell Daddy, did you have a bad dream?"

But Parri only stared at him and went on calling, "Daddy, Daddy. Please, Daddy."

"I'm here." Josh lifted her tenderly in his arms. The long white sheet trailed after her and Penny pulled it over her head.

"Look, Parri," she said gently. "Here's Mummie. Daddy's holding you and Mummie's right here. Look, darling, look at me."

Parri's frightened staring eyes held no sign of recognition. Her arms flailed the air and to keep her still Josh sat down on the low nursery rocker Penny pushed toward him. He smoothed back her hair and Penny dipped a corner of the snuggle bunny into a glass of water on the night table. "See?" she said, sponging gently, as Josh had done for her. "We're all here together. Here's Daddy, here's Mummie—and here's Dog. Say, 'Hi, Dog.' "

[64]

Parri's frantic vision began to focus and she drew in long sobbing breaths. Dog's loving tongue reached out to lick her bare toes and she let her hand drop so he could kiss it. "Dog," she quavered, and lay back.

"It was a bad old dream." The eyes of two frightened parents met above the tousled brown head, and Josh bent down to say, "But it's gone. It's all-l-l gone."

Parri lay still and looked around her. "The—Things are gone," she murmured. "Bad Things, Mummie."

"Yes, lamb."

They both wondered what Things could so trouble a little child, what terror could creep into a life kept so completely empty of fear; and Parri confused them further by saying, "They were all slick and funny. They ate Dog."

"No, they didn't. Dog's right here. He says, 'Woof-woof, Parri.'"

"They ate all of him and they tried to eat me. They *almost* ate me," she declared. Her inherited sense of drama was waking up with all her other senses, thirst, hunger, and the pleasure of being up at ten o'clock at night.

She was comfortably enthroned in her father's arms and held autocratic court there for half an hour. She held it until Trudy came home from her church meeting and ended the audience.

"Back you go," Trudy said, without even going on to her room to take off her hat and watching Penny remake the bed with quick precision. "I reckon, Mr. Josh, if you'll take her to the bathroom, we'll put her back in. She's had enough fun to pay for the inconvenience of a nightmare."

So Parri was back in her nest and Dog was coaxed down the stairs and out. This was his one free time of the day and he usually took a good snuffle through the woods and made it last as long as he could, but tonight he confined himself to a quick lope around the house and hurried inside and padded back to his mat in the hall.

"Do you suppose she isn't well?" Penny whispered through the dark, when she and Josh were in bed and he was almost asleep. "Do you think I should have taken her temperature? She didn't feel hot."

"I think she's all right, but if she's droopy in the morning, you might call Dr. Gray."

Parri was as chipper as the birds next morning. She had forgotten her dream but not the ensuing entertainment it had brought. "I had fun," she said at breakfast, when Penny wanted all her time for more talk with Josh. "Can I get up again tonight?"

"You may not." Josh tried to look stern over the top of his paper. When thirty-eight speaks to three, it is more awesome than the Commander-in-Chief of the armies reproving a private; and he had no idea that Parri stared back at him and thought he was a mean old man. "We're having house guests," he said, in what sounded to him like a pleasant explanatory tone and which was far more than he had ever received as a child. "Daddy wants you to show them what a good little girl you are."

"Tonight?" It was Penny who jumped to attention and upset the cream pitcher. "Oh, great stars above!" she cried. "It's only Friday and I thought Neda wouldn't be able to come until after tomorrow night's performance."

"She quit for a rest. I told you that, dear." He watched a yellow river send out tributaries for Joshua's ready hands to spat; and while he helped mop up with his napkin, he said,

[66]

"She was fed up with two years in a hit, so all she'll want will be a lot of sleep. You won't have to be fancy."

"But I'm not ready. Is Brooks coming, too?"

"Yep." Josh's napkin was soaked and dripping, so he squeezed what he could back into the pitcher and gave the cloth to the baby to suck on. "Keep him occupied," he said into Penny's uncertain frown. "Clean napkin, good country cream. All you have to do," he went on, above the flutter she made over moving a bowl of flowers and pushing plates and silver around, "is shove Joshu's crib in with Parri and turn the guest room back into the petunia bower it used to be."

"It's gray with white lilies, stupe. And where shall I put Brooks?"

"On the studio couch in our workroom. He can spread his stuff on a desk. He's a careless soul, anyway."

"Well. . . ." The table was a shambles so she dried her sticky hands on one corner of the cloth, and moaned, "Oh, dear me, I hadn't planned to go to market this morning. I'll just have to do it though, I guess." Then she stopped and looked at him. "What does presume mean?" she asked.

"Which one? The 'you're presuming on my hospitality' kind?"

"No." Penny missed the twinkle in his eyes for she was serious. "The other one. This is Mrs. Bandler's day to market—she always avoids the Saturday crush—and I always try to avoid her. I got her last week, so I told Carrol we'd go tomorrow. She's always *presuming* about me. 'You're having spinach today, I presume?' 'The children are well, I presume?' What does she mean?"

"That she thinks, hopes, supposes—I presume."

"Then why doesn't she say so? There's the spinach right

under her nose and I wouldn't be in town if the children were sick. Why doesn't she ever say 'I guess' or 'I expect,' just once?"

"Search me. Shall I presume to ask her?"

"No, I wouldn't wish it on my worst enemy." Penny pushed up the milky sleeves of her pink sweater and lapsed into revery while Josh returned to his damp newspaper. Now and then she muttered about barbecued steaks and extra bacon, or having to cut her roses, but the only real sounds were the sucking noises Joshu made.

When she had seen Josh off, she reversed the order of her day by not waiting for Carrol and by going to Mr. Bellow's first, while Mrs. Bandler and her chauffeur pushed aside the little people in the A & P. This was most inconvenient, since most of the items she needed were across the street and it was hard to plan dessert and salads for her menus until she knew what cuts of meat she could buy. She finally solved the problem by buying some of this and a lot of that; Apples for a pie, boxes of berries, a watermelon, peaches, avocados, "just in case"; soup, should the weather turn cold, melon if it were hot. She ordered ice cream to be delivered and a special rum cake that Mrs. Johns at the book store made. The back of her station wagon which was not as dapper as the one from Gladstone, having been bought second-hand during the shortage, was well loaded before she got to the solid foods that fill the inner man. Her wallet was much flatter, too, and but for a Travellers Check she carried for an emergency, she would have had to go to the bank. When she had it all in, when there was nothing more she could think of beyond a ham, steaks, a leg of lamb, assorted cold cuts, chickens, cheeses of many kinds, sweet potatoes, Irish potatoes, both new and old, with fresh vegetables to add to her own waning supply, she trundled it home and delivered it to Minna.

"There," she said, staggering under her last brown bag and dumping it on the kitchen table. "If you need anything more, don't ask me for it."

"Are you sure you have it all? You forgot your list again." Minna poked through the exhibit like a detective hunting for the missing clue while Penny sat on a stool in triumphant silence. "The butter," she reminded, in a happy voice that solved the case. "Did you bring the butter and eggs from Gladstone?"

"No, drat it, I forgot 'em." Penny wearily stretched out her legs and rested both hands on her knees. "Marketing's no joke," she grumbled. "Any man who thinks so—just let him try it. I'll get the darned old butter but I'd planned to do a lot of other things."

The drive to Gladstone took three minutes at the most, and when she turned in between two tall stone posts and shrubbery that hid a lodge house, she felt as young and happy as the first time she had done it. That had been eleven years ago. The Parrishes had just moved to West Point. Colonel Parrish was an instructor, David a cadet; and Carrol, proud to show her lovely home, had driven her over. To Penny, accustomed to an army house with a front yard and back, this half mile of woods and lawn and gardens was beyond belief; and when she saw the brick and stucco mass of turrets and towers that reared against the sky at the end of a winding drive she could only stare in stupefied silence. She still felt the same excited pleasure. Whenever her tires marked the neat gravel she became fifteen again, eager and a little vain over having this right of way to the portals of the rich. The only difference was that she never quite got over the surprise of having her brother live there.

David was such a steady, unassuming person. Trudy always pointed out that even as a small boy he knew where he was going, and went there. From a long, proud line of army officers he had turned out to be a farmer. He had seen a job to be done, rolling acres that needed to be worked, cattle improved. There was no one else to do it. Carrol's father was gone, and Gladstone could become either the plaything of an officer's rich wife, or sold. So he had resigned his commission, rolled up his sleeves, and made a good life for himself and his family.

He was on the stone terrace as Penny swept around the circular driveway, talking with a carpenter about new screens for the tall French windows, and he ran down the steps before a very correct butler could hurry out. "I'll take it, Perkins," he called back to the old man who had spent most of his life working for Carrol's family. "It's only the brat." Then he leaned in the open window and said, "Hi. Why don't you trade in this rattletrap?"

"We aren't so rich as some I know." Penny made a face at him and he made a face back.

His blue eyes laughed at her and his hair almost matched his faded tan jersey. David was straight of line and slim of hip, still whittled to a West Pointer's measurements, but war and little Davy's illness had etched fine lines on his face and his tussle with the land had bronzed it to a deep copper. "Carrol and Davy are down at the pool," he said. "Want to walk down?"

"I haven't time. I just came for some eggs and butter. I'm

in a frightful rush." And with that, she proceeded to spend half an hour telling him all the news she could think of, including her coming week end.

David leaned on the door and listened with amused brotherly interest; and when her dairy products had been brought out and the butter was melting on the seat beside her, he said, "Okay, we'll come over tonight if we can. Don't count on us for dinner though. Carrol wants to start back to the shore early tomorrow so we can't stay late either."

"And that looks as if I won't see you at all. A fine help you'll be!" Penny threw her car into gear and pushed his face out of her way. "This thing jumps," she warned. "No matter how careful I am, it—jumps."

She went off in a leap that spurted gravel back and left her no time to wave. Her morning was gone and she still had an endless number of things to do. She rode along and counted them until she ran out of fingers, then turned in at her own neat gate and her own stone house that was more beautiful to her than Gladstone.

By six o'clock she was ready. Parri looked like a red and white valentine in her new smocked dress, Joshu like a Schmoo in his night gown. She herself was the charming country hostess, very informal in pink linen, and very, very tired.

To keep Parri clean was a task, even after Joshu gave out and was put to bed, and she let her carry napkins out to the room. Trips were made with ice and canapés. Flies and little bugs got as sleepy as Joshu had and went off wherever they rest, and the fireflies waked. It was seven, then it was eight, and Parri reluctantly went the way of other small creatures. At nine o'clock, Penny stood on the lawn, hands on her hips and shouting through the kitchen window to Minna. "Go on upstairs," she yelled. "If they haven't sense enough to come at a respectable hour they can go to an inn for dinner. I could murder Josh." And she muttered to herself, "I know I said it. I meant to and I won't give him a dollar, either."

"I have not much to do if you cook outside," Minna called back, unusually cheerful because John sat in the kitchen with her, all decked out in a white serving coat. "We wait."

"We don't wait." Penny stalked around the house and was blinded by headlights. "Well, at *last!*" she jeered, then remembered her manners.

Josh slid out first, and under cover of kissing her, growled, "Had to wait while Neda packed. Slow? Ye gods!" And Penny smiled with all irritation forgotten while she made happy gestures of welcome.

Neda Thayne was a tall girl with red-gold hair, and Brooks Cameron was much too fat and had an owlish look because of horn rimmed glasses and a center part in his thinning hair. They came out of the coupé like chickens shaking their feathers when released from a coop, and Penny disliked herself for being glad they had had an uncomfortable trip.

"Nice place you have," Brooks said, pumping her hand. He had been at Round Tree Farm many times and always made the same remark, so she patted his wrinkled back and told him to leave his coat on the porch, then turned to Neda.

"Hello," she greeted again, eagerly, "I'm awfully glad you could come, and congratulations on the part in the play. Don't you love it?"

"Umhum." Neda knew she had the part only because Penny had refused it. She knew, too, that the girl facing her

[72]

was the better actress, so shrugged and defended, "If it doesn't fail. I gave up something sure for it."

"It won't." Penny linked their arms together and went on in companionable woman-to-woman talk, "I was getting lonesomer by the minute while I waited. I had a million things I wanted to talk to you about, but now I can't remember a one. Golly, I'm glad you came."

She watched Josh take two cases from the car, a small shabby one that belonged to Brooks and a hand trunk that was large enough to hold quite a wardrobe; and when he had given them to John, she suggested, "Let's go out to the room. You can relax while Josh broils steaks. He thinks it's fun to cook."

"Poor dear, he shouldn't have to when he's so tired." Neda looked proprietary as she pulled back and waited. She was hooked to Penny but she waited for Josh with almost wifely concern and helped him out of his jacket with her free hand.

Penny was too happy to notice. Her work was finished and country entertaining had turned into fun. She loved the soft glow of lights through the windows, the black velvet lawn, the gleam of hurricane lamps and dim outline of tables and chairs in the room, the damp kiss of night on her face; and best of all, she loved the pride in it that Josh shared with her. "I'll take his coat," she said without thinking, expecting to toss it carelessly into the porch. But Neda kept it.

"I may slip it on if it gets cool," she answered, releasing herself and dropping back so Penny and Brooks walked ahead.

The air was cool and quiet in the room. Josh unhooked his skillet from the wall and put on his mannish white apron. There was little for him to do, for the fire in the pit before the wall was a bed of bright coals, but he took his steaks from a small refrigerator beside it and laid them on the grill. Penny thought of going to help him but saw Neda already there, watching him drop potatoes into a frying pan, so she drifted over to Brooks and stretched out in a canvas deck chair beside him.

He grinned at her, then his eyes strayed to Neda. Josh had come back to the table for cigarettes and she leaned against the sink waiting for him, a splotch of bright color in shadow. Her cheeks were flushed, her golden hair flamed with the firelight. "Tell me," he asked. "Don't you mind giving that babe over there *carte blanche?*"

"No." Penny answered with confidence and seemed to miss his meaning. "Josh thinks she can do the part. He says he'll have to make some changes of course, because he had me in mind at first, but he'll pull her through. Josh," she said proudly, "can turn Neda into Anne."

But what can she do to him? he wondered. He had had a brush or two with Neda's wiles and knew of several others, two of whom had been her husbands. The child beside him was no match for Neda Thayne—especially if she stuck to the country and her mother role. Neda liked to grab the spotlight and she was a better actress off the stage than on, or at least a more profitable one. Two matrimonial ventures had paid off well and she could afford a third with nothing more to gain than love or being the wife of a top-notch producer. She was working at it now and had been while she took her time to pack.

Brooks had sat in her handsome mirrored living room, reading a copy of *The New Yorker* while Josh was invited to the other side of the door where boudoir pillows and perfume bottles cluttered the place. He had tried to keep his mind on his reading, as any good chaperon should, but scraps of conversation drifted out and they weren't always too closely tied up with the play. Neda's great loneliness kept creeping in, her fear of failure and her beautiful trust in Josh. "You're giving me the only real chance I've ever had," he heard. "You'll help me, won't you? *Will* you come up here and help me, where I won't be so self-conscious and timid?" No wonder it took her so long to toss a few clothes together.

Brooks remembered Josh's final promise and turned his head to look at the dim, relaxed line of Penny. She looked such a neatly brushed little girl; just lying there, quite contented for Neda to smile at Josh over the salad she probably had made, to pop a big black cherry into his mouth and laughingly hold her hand under his chin for the seed. Penny didn't even see it, for at that moment she stretched her arms above her head and said contentedly, "This is when the country's lovely, Brooks. When we have our friends out and mix our work with play." Then Josh called that the steaks were almost ready and she got up to take charge.

"Tired, darling?" she asked, taking four plates with slices of melon from the refrigerator and pushing a button that brought John on the run with hot rolls.

"Bushed. Where do you want Neda to sit?"

"On your right, where she can look out at the fireflies. Brooks, you come around here." She moved the hurricane lamps from a shelf above the sink and set them on the table. "Thanks, Neda," she said gratefully, "for helping. My feet enjoyed the rest."

For a few minutes talk centered around food and peaceful quiet of the country versus New York's rackety life. Each one listened to another's argument but would never cede a point of his own and Neda was the first to tire of it. She watched Penny get up to help John serve the steaks and kept Josh still with her hand on his sleeve. "I've been meaning to ask you, Josh," she said, "and keep forgetting it. Do you really want me to know my lines before our first rehearsal?"

"Not *know* them," he answered, "but I do want you to be able to really read them. Jervis is tough and you can't go in there with him, cold."

"He always told me that, too." Penny put Josh's plate before him and smoothed the rough top of his hair. "You've got yourself a slave driver, friend," she said. "He almost ruined my honeymoon." Then she went back to her stove.

"But there's so little time," Neda protested, just as if Penny hadn't been there. "Fritz hasn't finished the rewrite job, so how can I do it?"

"The first act's the same and most of the third. I'll cue you."

"Tonight?" She leaned closer, but Penny was back.

"And how!" Penny informed her, gently pushing her hand away to set down a salad. "Tonight, all day tomorrow, and if you don't give out, tomorrow night, too. But I'll save you. I'll declare a rest period every so often and give Brooks a chance to talk about his props." She went around the table, punched the drowsy Brooks, and whispered, "Don't let the country air get you," then sat down at her own place. "This is fun," she said, beaming benignly on them all. "But if you're planning to work you'd better eat fast. I've had a long hard day and I'm apt to get sleepy."

Brooks pulled himself up in his chair and wondered what

she thought she had to do with it, asleep or awake, and soon
found out. She helped him turn the living room into a stage.
She knew where every chair belonged as well as he or Josh
did, where the imaginary stairway should be and the exits;
and she tugged screens and stools from the kitchen to mark
them. And when everything was ready, she seated herself on
the floor in the hall archway and prepared to be a critical
audience.

"I can't do it," Neda protested petulantly, finding the whole
situation out of hand and two too many people involved. "I'd
rather sit and read it first. Just Josh and I."

"You've already done that." Penny took charge again instead of letting the director decide. She tucked her feet under
her and looked very permanent as she said, "This is the way
we always do it. Sometimes even Carrol and David watch,
and they love it when the going gets rough. I won't talk,
though," she promised. "I'll go away after a bit and make
coffee."

She slid over to rest her back against the white casing and
Neda looked at her helplessly. An audience in itself was no
great hindrance, for she was accustomed to working with
people dodging about in the way; it was this special one. It
was Penny. Penny, the real actress, the real Anne, the real
McCoy. She sat down on the divan.

"Not me," she said. "I won't do it."

Josh sensed her difficulty. He knew he couldn't do it,
either, in Neda's place; not with those big eyes watching him,
hiding their knowledge of his inadequacy but showing dis-
may when he fumbled and misfired. Penny was quite apt to
jump up and throw herself into the act. She would do it with

the best intentions; and much as he hated to, he had to step in. "Listen, Pen," he said, "I see Neda's point. She isn't ready for this yet."

"She's *worked* on the part, hasn't she?"

"Yes, but not like we go at things. You and I know how to work together. Neda isn't used to that. I can see how she might be upset by you watching, so perhaps you'd better not stay tonight."

"Oh." Penny sat quite still. She looked at Victory-en-throned-on-the-couch, then up at her troubled husband. "Please," Josh's eyes were saying. "Please understand, darling," and she unfolded herself and got up. "All right," she decided, accepting her dismissal. "I'll borrow Brooks for the evening."

"Tomorrow we'll let you see what we've done." It was like patting Parri when she was sent off to bed, and Josh hated it. For one mad moment he was tempted to hurl his script at Penny, to shout, "Come back here! Come back here and get on the set where you belong! This whole darned business is your fault!" But he only stood and watched her cross the hall.

Saturday followed the same pattern. Minna had restored the living room to its immaculate order and children and Dog were underfoot, so Josh and Neda retired to the room. They were visible but inviolate, and Penny served them their lunch but brought the dining room into unaccustomed use for dinner. She fussed over upstairs ventilation when Brooks was invited to a conference on the porch, and until she got him back, followed Trudy into her room.

"Are you having fun, child?" Trudy asked, knowing she wasn't.

"No." Penny made no pretense. "Business belongs in town where I don't have to see it," she said. "Josh's week ends ought to belong to me."

"Not when he has to work so hard. Miss Neda's a mighty pretty girl, but from what I've seen through the kitchen window she don't know much more about actin' than Dog does. Seems like I've heard Mr. Josh say her speeches for her so many times I know 'em by heart. Is they about through?"

"As far as I can see, they never will be." Penny watched her inspect a ruffle on a pair of Parri's white nainsook panties and take a needle out of the heartshaped cushion David had made and stuffed when he had the mumps. "He'll go on and on until he's satisfied, I guess, I presume."

"You could have been in Miss Neda's shoes, child, so don't grumble."

"I'm not, and it's too late anyway if I am," Penny answered, looking lugubrious. "Josh said tonight she's improving."

"Then let's be grateful for that and hope she won't backslide tomorrow."

"Tomorrow? Ha-ha! If I live till bedtime tomorrow night I hope I never hear the word theater again! I wish Josh would go into the ditch-digging business. I don't think I can *last* until tomorrow."

But she did. After she had seen her guests off in the coupé with Josh saying he'd take the bus to town in the morning, she let him help her up the stairs with both hands under her elbows and a push on every step. And she heard the hated word theater over and over.

"We get the *Fulton* theater a week from tomorrow," he said, yawning and jerking off his tie, but still full of enthusiasm. *"Love in the Spring"* comes in ten days later and I'll have to find some other place to rehearse. Lots of shows are closed for August so I can pick another theater. Make a note on your scratch pad, Pen, will you? Remind me to call Pierce about the Philadelphia try out. I almost feel as if we might open," he said cheerfully.

Penny slipped off her pumps and hobbled to the telephone calendar. *"Phone Jeb Pierce,"* she wrote, as Josh went happily on:

"Perhaps we can have Fritz out next week, too. Then if we find any bugs left in the thing we'll take 'em out and pull it together."

"Oh, Josh, *no!"* She sent the words out in a wail. She howled louder than Dog with a thorn in his paw. "I can't take it again!" she cried. "I'm worn out! I've washed dishes, carried trays, made beds, kept the children out of the way, and myself, too, just like the wife of a big executive. And I've been patronized, forgotten, ignored, shunned, dismissed, vetoed. . . ."

"Poor baby."

"Until I feel like a proposal the Russians have kicked around."

"It won't happen next week." Josh disappeared into his closet that had drawers and a clothes rod and served him as a dressing cabinet, and called back, "Neda's doing fine."

"At what?"

Her face was innocently bland when he came out in his pajamas, and he pulled her up and kissed her roughly. "At lots of things, you fool," he said. "Sometime I'll tell you."

He gave her a spank that sent her galloping across the

room and shortened her nightly ablutions to record time. And while she was brushing her hair in a happy hit-a-lick fashion, he said, "It doesn't make sense."

"What doesn't?" Penny paused with lifted brush.

"You. Having you on the sidelines while I work without you. It's a mess, Mrs. MacDonald." He punched his pillow higher and clasped his hands behind his head, enjoying her stare and the way her mouth stayed a little open. She looked like a ruffly baby bird that didn't get the worm it expected. "But I like it," he said, giving in, "I honestly do. I think you're cute."

CHAPTER V

PENNY drove Josh to the village next morning, and while they waited in front of the drug store, she remarked, "I feel as if I'm sending a nice present to Neda—neatly wrapped in a gray suit and tied with a hand-painted scarf from Sulka's."

"Too bad you can't come along and present me in person," he returned amiably. "It ought to be fun. 'Many happy returns of the day, Miss Thayne. I brought you my husband. He's badly worn in spots but fairly durable, just a little old second-hand husband and not a real antique. If you're careful of him he'll last you a lifetime.' "

They both laughed, Penny a little ruefully, as the big Greyhound bus hummed toward them. "Well, good-by, kiddo," he said, keeping it light and giving her a quick kiss before he swung out to the curb. "See you between seven and midnight."

He waved as the heavy automatic door closed behind him, then walked back along the aisle to a seat. Halfway he stopped, peered over a newspaper and said to David Parrish, "Well, of all people to meet! What are you doing here?"

"Hi." David lowered his paper and motioned with it. "Park," he invited. "I came back from the shore last night. Just took the station wagon up to Highland Falls to have an appendectomy done on it and decided to see a guy down the line about some feed while I waited. I'm getting off at the next stop."

"Did Carrol come home, too?" Josh dropped into the aisle

chair, adjusted the back to his comfort as David answered:

"No, she's determined to finish the month out. She thinks salt water's good for Davy. How's the theatrical business?"

"Due to your sister, it's shot to blazes." Josh grinned to soften his words, but David snatched at the remark.

"I've been wanting to stick my finger in that pie," he said. "What's the matter with Pen, anyway? Why isn't she pulling her half of the load?"

"She is."

"Not when she's letting you down. You're a team—you started out as a team. Why, good Lord, she almost drove us crazy until she got to be an actress. Then she popped into your life and got herself all tangled up with it, and now she's quitting. I don't like it."

"Well," Josh pulled a rumpled newspaper from his pocket and laid it across his knees, "I do," he answered. "In a way, it parallels your life with Carrol. Women are meant to be wives and mothers. Girl babies are given a doll to play with the minute they're able to hold a toy. Boys get Erecto sets and trains, and girls get dolls and houses with little furniture, electric stoves, and an ironing board with an iron that really presses. It isn't a matter of training, Dave, it's what they like. Parri stumbled right over a train last Christmas to get to a doll in a high chair."

"Yeah, but Penny didn't play with dolls much as a kid," David protested. "She liked Teddy bears better. She liked to dress up and put on plays, too," he added, when Josh looked too fondly amused. "And anyway, how does all this tie in with Carrol?"

"You're a farmer," Josh explained, serious now, "but you don't expect Carrol to go out every morning and oversee the ploughing. If she wants to ride her hunter around the fields with you, just for pleasant company and good exercise, fine, you like it; but if she wants to run the house and take care of the kids and buy groceries, that suits you, too. She doesn't *have* to plough. Penny doesn't either."

"I get you." David was silent a moment, then stood up. "Here's where I leave you," he said, pushing past Josh's knees. Then he leaned on the seat in front of him. "Women beat the Dutch, don't they?"

"They sure do."

Josh watched him swing off the bus and cross the wide village street before he unfolded his *Herald Tribune* that had the crossword puzzle torn out. He doubted if David would accept his explanation of Penny's behavior and decided to take time off at lunch to warn her of a visitor. He made a neat mental note for a telephone date with her, then looked down at the ragged printed page and hoped she would save the puzzle so he could finish the editorial it had on its back.

Penny lost the puzzle before she got home. It blew off the seat and floated away on the breeze. She felt sad about it. Something unfinished was flying away. Someone, she told herself, had worked hard to make that puzzle, perhaps had sat up all night. "I'm sorry, dear," he had said to his wife, "but I can't go to the movies. I've got a deadline to meet and I can't think of one darned word for seventeen across that will fit in with seventeen down." There he sat, hunched over, his poor eyes red and tired, needing glasses. He was hot and miserable in his box of an apartment and the baby made snuffling noises in the next room. Poor little Junior wouldn't have milk if his daddy didn't finish the puzzle. "Oh, please, God," he prayed, thumbing pages in the dictionary, "help me. Let people like my puzzles. Let just one person write me a fan letter so I can keep my job. *'Dear Sir; your puzzles are wonderful. I like them because. . . .'*" Penny stopped the car and backed up.

There was no sign of a quarter-page from the *Herald Tribune* beside the road, even though she backed a long way. Tin cans, bottles, remains of picnic lunches littered the shallow ditch, but no puzzle. "It's meant to be," she decided. "I'll never know the man's name, but perhaps a tramp will find it. He'll be tired and lonely and can sit on the bank with something nice to entertain him. It will probably make him remember when he was a little boy and lovely unexpected things happened to him. Maybe he found a dime and bought a book to color, and crayons; or perhaps his mother went marketing and brought him a present."

"Present" reminded her of Josh whom she had sent off to Neda, and she let the tramp and puzzle-maker to do the best they could for themselves while she worried over her own husband. "I'm certainly making it tough for him," she muttered, going forward again. "I wish I knew if I'm doing the right thing about me."

She considered the problem all week. She worried it as Dog did a bone; gnawing on it a while, burying it, then digging it up again. David's call and scolding which would have seemed accidental but for Josh's warning, did nothing to help her. Nor did Josh's noncommittal replies to her questions about Neda. "She's doing all right," he would say. "How about driving in to Henderson's for some ice cream?"

And Carrol, who was something like a pin cushion for all the troubles Penny stuck into her without ever showing the holes, stayed down at the shore.

The second week end rolled around and the house was ahum with Josh's gang. Penny sought the privacy of her bathroom which was the only place she ever could count on to be alone, and leaned her forehead against the cool tile beside the shower. "Oh, dear," she groaned. "What's wrong with me? I know I'm doing the right thing . . . I decided so in cold, calm logic. I was happy about it and contented. I was *quite* contented," she repeated. "Now, I'm not. What's *wrong?*"

There was no one to tell her. Trudy had said all she intended to say, all she knew Penny's mother would want her to say, and seemed to take pleasure in what she called "the ructions of a bunch of crazy people." Less rehearsing was being done so there was more conversation that left Penny out. Arguments cropped up over technicalities about which she knew nothing; joking references were made to incidents that left her blank; and she felt like "it" in a game of blind man's buff. Whenever she managed to catch someone, the victim slithered away and she was left clutching empty air.

Neda had become very sure of herself. She tossed in cozy little remarks like, "Josh, you wretch, the other evening when you were up, you left a cigarette burn on my end table." And over dinner in the room, she said, "It's going to be hard if Josh ever stops paying my expenses. He feeds me all my meals in town and gives me board and room in the country."

Penny didn't like the *"if* Josh stops paying." She preferred "when," for there was no doubt in her mind that Josh would stop after the play opened; but she only said graciously, "Don't worry, pet, we'll put you up box lunches."

"Meow," Brooks leaned over to whisper. "Your claws drew blood." And that was the first time she felt that any of them had even heard her voice.

"I must lift it oftener," she told herself; and promptly tried it by suggesting, "Josh, if I come to town on Monday will you take me to lunch and let me watch the first real rehearsal in a theater?"

The amused look Neda gave her was so sharp it made her blush. It said very plainly, "So you *are* afraid," and made her hastily amend, "If I can finish my shopping in time, I mean. I do have a lot to buy."

She was suddenly ashamed of herself. I hate me, she thought turbulently. I never used to make cracks and try to show off. I'm becoming a disgusting person. And she cut off Josh's, "Sure, honey," by saying honestly, "I don't know what made me ask that. I couldn't go in town on Monday any more than I can fly. I was just feeling left out, I guess."

"You're never left out." Josh smiled down the table at her and shook his head. "Not purposely, Pen. Sometimes we get to talking and forget you, but we don't mean to."

"Thank you." Penny went through the rest of the week end like a banner in the breeze. Josh was hers, he had said so right before them all; and whenever the wind died down and left her drooping, she blew herself out again with her own courage.

And so the period of preparation ended and the play was put in rehearsal.

At first Josh came home like a boy from the circus, talking

a mile a minute and showing the prizes he had won in a box of cracker jack. Everything was fine; the cast was great and shook right down into their parts; changes in the play were just what it needed; dates in Philadelphia clicked; the scenery was coming along great guns. Then suddenly he became quiet. Praise slackened and he wore the harried frown Penny knew so well from working with him in other productions. He came home later and later, and crawled wearily into bed.

"It's all right, honey,—I guess," he said, when his rehearsals had moved from the *Fulton* to the *Empire,* and throwing himself into the swing. "We'll make it."

"Josh, is Neda. . . ."

"She's doing okay. I've just got the jitters."

Penny sat on the edge of a cushion and smoothed his hair. She wanted to ask more questions but he said, "Find me a cigarette and light it, will you? Traffic was awful tonight. I thought I'd never get home."

"You shouldn't have tried." She got up, took a cigarette from a box on the table and got it going with a great deal of wasted effort and shooting sparks. "Here," she said, putting it between his upraised fingers. "Perhaps you shouldn't come home at night until after the play opens."

"I'd rather." He drew in a few contented breaths and pulled her down beside him. "This rests me," he sighed, turning on his side and laying his head in her lap. "When I'm tired clear through to my bones, I tell myself how swell it will be when I get home to you. I find myself hurrying to get here."

But two nights later he didn't come home at all.

Joshu had the sniffles and Penny had spent the day plugging in the croup kettle and trying to keep him entertained in his bed. At seven o'clock she got him into a wheezy sleep, then made a hasty toilet and took her station on the porch where she could hear any sound through a window above her. Dusk settled down in a businesslike way that said the sky had shut up shop for the night and the world would have to get on as best it could without a moon for a lantern. Car headlights flashed at the intersection, and she jumped up whenever they lighted her road, only to watch them pass her open, hospitable gate. When Minna brought out a tray and put it on a low table before her chair, she pushed it away and went inside to telephone.

Josh still kept an apartment in New York. It was a relic of his bachelor days and was a small shabby affair that he and Penny often used when she was working, and during the past year it had become his office. Neither had bothered to make it attractive for they liked its stark simplicity after a cluttered day; and as she gave its number, she could see the hideous Axminster rug, the worn leather chairs, and knew it was empty long before the operator gave up ringing and told her it was.

"I wouldn't fret, child," Trudy said, coming into the little library behind the stairs and laying a soothing hand on Penny's slumped shoulders. "I reckon he's on his way home."

"Not without telephoning me first." Penny shook her head. "He always calls at dinnertime when he's going to be late."

"Try some other places."

"I did. I tried the *Athletic Club,* the *Lambs Club*—I even tried the *Union League,* though he doesn't belong. And I tried *Sardi's,* and *Toots Shor's,* and *Twenty One.* I thought Neda might drag him to *Twenty One,* but she hadn't."

"Then you'd best eat your supper and wait."

"I can't." Penny looked at the croup kettle Trudy had re-filled and it might have been a basket of flowers for all she cared. "I'll have to go to town," she said.

"Child, you can't, at this late hour."

"I'll have to."

Trudy unwound the cord around the kettle, straightened it out, then slowly wound it back again. "Did you try Miss Neda's apartment?" she asked, and Penny nodded.

"Yes, and no one answered there either, though I prayed Josh would. No one answers at the theater or anywhere else, so I'll have to go hunt him."

"Among seven million people? How do you expect to find him?"

"I don't know." Penny leaned forward and rested her head against the stiff white front of Trudy's apron. "Wherever he is," she said, "he needs me." Then she looked up, her face strained. "Nothing else matters much when Josh needs me. Nothing else *dares* matter. I promised to love him and cherish him—and I'm not doing it very well. The children have you. You stayed here with me when Mums went to Germany so I'd be free to do all the things I promised to do, and yet I haven't done them. Trudy . . ." Her arms reached around the sturdy waist with its white bow at the back . . . "have I been awfully selfish?" she asked.

"No, child, just a little slow at discoverin' that Mr. Josh ain't got the same wife he married. He loved you as you was and he loves you as you is. Maybe he loves you more as you is, Miss Penny."

"I don't think so. He wouldn't stay away from me tonight if he did. There's some reason why he's staying away."

Penny straightened up. She pushed the telephone back to its proper place on the table and said briskly, "I hope that fool station wagon will keep its heart pumping till I get there."

"You ain't drivin' off in that rattletrap, you just ain't."

"Not if John drives me?"

"Not even so." Trudy could be as determined as Penny and more practical. "When a girl waits to the very end of the limit to untangle a tangle, a few more minutes ain't goin' to matter," she pointed out. "You've been hidin' from New York for a good many weeks and it won't miss you tonight."

"I'll catch the bus." Penny stood up and her chin trembled in spite of the firm way her lips were pressed together. The white enameled croup kettle was a reminder of her sick baby upstairs and she half reached for it, then drew her hands back. "You don't think he has much fever, do you?" she whispered.

"I don't think he has any now, child."

"If he should have, you know how to melt half an aspirin in a teaspoon of water and to give him an alcohol rub. And if Parri should have a bad dream. . . ."

"Miss Penny, won't you wait till tomorrow?"

"No." Penny walked out in the hall and took her heavy white coat from the closet. "I'll have to go right now to catch the ten o'clock bus. If John's gone to bed, I'll leave the car by the drug store." She found her patent leather purse on a shelf and slipped its long strap over her shoulder. "If Josh should call. . . ." She stopped and sighed. "He won't," she said. "Poor darling, he's forgotten all about it."

John's light was on above the garage and he came down when she called. "Kind of foolish, ain't you?" he asked, coaxing the station wagon to life. "Traipsin' off at this hour of night?"

Penny shook her head. She had been wanting to talk with John about Minna and here was her beautiful chance, shut up alone with him where he couldn't elude her, but she only sat in silence. Josh, where are you? her thoughts cried. Where *are* you, darling, and will I be able to make you believe how I've changed when I find you?

The short way seemed endless even though John drove the station wagon at a surprising pace. The big bus was already at its appointed stop and the driver was just coming from the drug store, wiping a last bite of sandwich from his mouth. Penny paid him her fare and pulled herself up the steps. She found a seat in the middle, across from two giggling girls who talked untiringly and much as she had after a date at West Point; and since a breeze came in, she pulled her coat around her shoulders and snuggled down into it. Dark miles flashed by. The girls' high voices changed to whispers and sometimes they glanced at her then put their heads together and whispered again. Penny was too busy with her own thoughts to notice, but when one leaned across the aisle and spoke to her, she turned.

"We were just wondering," the girl said, pretty, with a ripe, too-red mouth, "that is . . . It sounds kind of silly, but we have a bet on."

"Yes?" Penny tried to focus her attention but she had just remembered that Josh sometimes went to see Martin Goss who was a very good friend and had directed her first play. He might have gone there for advice. So she looked vague as the girl giggled and said:

"My friend here, Marion, thinks you're Penny Parrish.

THE RELUCTANT HEART

It sounds awfully dumb to me, because of course you *couldn't* be Penny Parrish, way out here and riding on a bus, so I bet her a dollar. We saw her last year in a play and you *do* look like her but. . . ."

"I am." Penny sent a smile across. "I'm sorry you lost," she said, "but I am. I live out here in the country."

"Oh." It was hard to tell if they were glad or disappointed because they only looked surprised; but the one named Marion leaned out and added, "Gee whizz. Imagine!"

There was a small flurry while they rustled about in their purses, then a crumpled paper napkin that had served as cleansing tissue was pushed across the aisle and Penny wrote her autograph under a smear of lipstick. She wrote it on a bus schedule, too. "Thanks," the girls said, seemingly content and through with her, leaving her free to think again.

She almost wished they would go on talking. Thinking, unless the thoughts are pleasant, is such a lonely way to travel; and she was glad to see the bright span of lights that marked the George Washington Bridge and to cross above the broad swift Hudson. Upper Manhattan flashed by. Harlem, bright and noisy, Columbus Circle with its determined soapbox orator, and glimpses through side streets of garish, sparkling Broadway. The bus came to a stop in its terminal. The few passengers who were left crowded to the door and the two girls got up and said a casual good-by.

"Good-by," Penny answered, and knew they were disappointed in her. She had no glamour. Her country coat and dotted dress were incorrect for New York night life, and, with transportation on a bus, were never meant for the *Stork Club.* She was just one of the seven million people Trudy had mentioned, and she walked out of the Greyhound station wondering how she was to find the six-million-nine-hundred-and-ninety-nine-thousandth one.

Even a loquacious taxicab driver was no help. He toured her to spots she already had telephoned and waited while she made more calls in drug stores. "Listen, lady," he said at last, "why don't you give up and go home? You could wait there for your husband. Guys have to go home *sometime*— I do, myself, in about half an hour."

"I hate to." Penny sat in the cab with the door open and asked, "Where would you go, if you were sort of unhappy and worried?"

"Well," the cab driver had an idea that sounded amusing to him, and he said, "I sure wouldn't go home to my old lady, that's certain. I'd go to see my girl. Has he got a girl?" No answer came from behind him and he slewed around to look through the opened glass partition, and repeated his question.

"I wish he had," Penny answered. "I'd know what to do, then."

"Well, make up your mind. I have to turn in my cab."

"All right." She slammed the door and sat back. "I'll go home," she said. "It's a place for me to be when he comes." She gave the address on east Thirty-seventh street and counted the short downtown blocks as they went by. "Between Park and Lexington," she said, when no more were left. "The big apartment over there with the marquee. You've been awfully nice to me."

"It's all in a day's work and we get queerer ones than you." He grinned at her as he clicked off his meter. "Some of 'em, believe it or not, ride around to keep a husband or wife from tailin' 'em, and some. . . ." But Penny had pressed a ten dollar bill in his hand.

"Thank you," she said, and walked slowly across the sidewalk.

Her key was in her purse, the key that fitted an inside door, and she found it and slipped it into the lock. The long T shaped hall was hot and stuffy after the cool air outside, and she slid out of her coat. The self-service elevator ground slowly upward but passed the floors too quickly for her and opened its doors with a rattle. Apartment 8A was down the hall and around a righthand turn. Penny traversed the tiled corridor with hesitant steps. She was a stranger. She was a strange woman coming to Josh's apartment in the early hours of morning; coming furtively, creeping along as if she had no right there. She had forgotten in all these many months what color the tiles were, what color the walls were painted. Her hand reached out and touched rough cream plaster. They were green, she thought. I'm sure they were green, and smooth.

The door was brown, it had been gray, and her key turned unwillingly in its lock. It rasped out a cross complaint as she turned the knob.

The little foyer was quite dark. A faint glow from a corner street lamp touched the ugly rug and marked a path past a work table and one of the fat, worn chairs. Penny moved across it and reached for an electric switch that would flood the whole small apartment with blazing, unkind light.

"Penny?" a voice said, and stopped her hand. "Is that you?"

"Y-yes." Josh's voice came from over by a window. It

[95]

sounded as if she might just have stepped out to do the marketing, and it made her wait to release her breath.

"I tried to call you," he said, "but the line was busy. Then I forgot. I'm sorry you were worried and had to come in."

"It doesn't matter, darling." She let her purse and coat fall and tiptoed across the room. "I should have come a long time ago," she said, standing beside him. "I didn't want to then; but I did—tonight." A battered leather footstool was near his chair and she pulled it to her and sat down on it, as close to him as she could manage. "Josh," she asked softly, "have we any extra money at all?"

"Not much that I know of, why?"

"I want to buy Neda's contract back, or whatever one does. I just found out tonight that I have to be in the play. I want to be," she said, when he was silent. "I want to be with you, and working. The children aren't enough. I found that out, too. Nothing's enough when we aren't together, when I'm not a part of you. Can you see that?"

"Yes, I see it, dear." He laid his hand over the hesitant fingers that touched his knee but turned his face to the lonely night outside. "I appreciate it, Pen," he said. "It isn't necessary, though. I'll work out something else tomorrow."

"Work out something else? Why?" She leaned closer until she could reach out and turn him back to her with her hand pushing his cheek, then she asked, "Josh, what are you talking about? What happened today?"

"Don't you know?"

"Of course, I don't know. How could I, stuck out in the hills like an ostrich, when you don't come home to tell me? What was it?"

"Brooks didn't call you?"

"No one called me. But I've called everyone I could think of and they must all be out on the town: Fritz, Neda, Brooks—Uncle Dad Goss was at home but he hadn't heard from you in a week. What happened?"

Josh bent over and kissed her. "Thanks, darling," he said with his arms around her, knowing that Penny always told him the absolute truth. "Thanks for coming. It's all right now."

"What is?"

"Neda quit," he said, with his lips against her hair, "or got fired, or whatever you want to call it. She was so lousy we couldn't go on. I thought you knew and came running. When you said you just found out tonight that you had to be in the play—gosh, I couldn't have let you do that, Pen."

"You dear stupid goat." Relief swept over Penny like a beautiful white-crested wave. Who, she thought, can say that some forms of sacrifice aren't fun? Anything which stops fear is lovely. And she pushed Josh back into his chair and crossed her arms on his knees. "Now listen, my friend," she scolded, "I'm sort of mad at you. Am I your wife, or am I an acquaintance? Now don't answer," she went on before he could speak. "I'm your wife. And you hadn't any right to keep your business to yourself. Where were you anyway?" she broke off to ask.

"I had dinner with Fritz in some joint. He got sore and told me I'd ruined him, and I left him there. After that. . . ." He stopped and shook his head. "I walked, I guess," he said. "I walked down to Washington Square and sat on a bench. Then I heard some sort of racket in a basement night club somewhere and went in for a while, and walked some more. I just walked."

[97]

"Didn't it ever occur to you to walk yourself toward home?"

"Most of the time, but I couldn't. I couldn't make up any sort of story that would keep you from seeing what a tough spot I'm in and flinging yourself to the rescue."

His hair was in worse confusion than usual with its black lock hanging over his forehead, and he looked so tired in the dim light that Penny fumbled around in his pocket. "Here," she said, taking out a crumpled package and his lighter. "Have a cigarette. Do we still keep milk in our refrigerator?"

"Nope, not any more."

"We always have milk in the country," she remarked smugly, and snapped the lighter open.

She was suddenly hungry. Her body had taken a long journey without fuel and was beginning to complain noisily, but she only hunched her knees higher and pressed her stomach into compact pleats that fooled it and made it stop fussing. Now was her turn to give to Josh: Not consolation and tender coddling, but comradely, matter-of-fact planning, easy and light; and she settled down to do it.

"Tell me," she said, knowing that talking it out would be good for him, and curious too, "how did you and Neda happen to part?"

"It's been coming ever since we started. She wasn't so bad when she first read the part for me, but the minute she hit the stage she turned brittle. Smartly brittle, which Anne isn't." He moved his cigarette from her head that kept nodding into it, and said carefully, "I think she honestly tried; but, Pen, Neda's a pretty determined sort of a gal. Perhaps she really wanted out, I don't know. Her contract had a two-week rehearsal clause in it that let us part by mutual agreement after a whale of a fight. I hated it most for the rest of the company because they've given their best and had a rough time."

"Do you think they'll mind having me come in so late and having to start all over again?"

"They'll welcome you like healing sunshine." He stubbed out his cigarette in an ash tray on the window sill before giving her a long searching look and asking the question she had hoped they could skip. "What made you really decide on this? Why tonight—at just this critical moment?"

There it was. Even if her whole system cried aloud in its hunger, she had to sit back and think how to answer. There were several ways. To tell him she loved him so much that she ran to him when her baby was sick, was wrong. It was true, but it was wrong. He would put that down to panic, not sensible reasoning, and would take her home. To say she loved acting so much that she had to come back, was equally silly. She did but she didn't, and he knew it. Penny gazed steadily back at Josh while she considered and rejected several explanations. None of them was any good, and she said at last, "I don't know. Everything got all mixed up together. It was sort of like cooking something, I guess. More things got put in the pot, more and more things, till the whole mess boiled over. I just blew the lid and got on a bus."

It was a garbled comparison but he seemed to understand it. "That's just about what life is, darling," he said, standing up and pulling her with him. "A large boiled dinner. It's after three o'clock, so what do you say we knock off? Rehearsal was called for ten before Neda and I went to the mat and we'll have to make it."

"Dear me, I haven't a nightgown." Penny knew she had got off lightly. Someday she would explain her complicated feelings to Josh, when the children were safely grown and she could look back and say gayly, "Wasn't I a goose to be afraid of leaving them?" but at that moment she welcomed the necessary fuss of moving furniture and pulling two beds out of the wall.

The room looked like a second hand furniture store when they finished; and she went into the foyer that had a Pullman kitchen on one side, neatly concealed behind white doors, and a large bathroom on the other. A chest of drawers in the bathroom gave up two sheets and a torn pair of pajamas for Josh. "I'll sleep in my slip," she yawned, putting a half-folded sheet on each bed and crawling wearily between hers. "I think Mr. Shakespeare had something."

"What?"

"Much Ado about Nothing." She took the hand Josh held out to her and snuggled down with it under her cheek. " 'Night, dearest," she said, and lay listening to his even breathing that told her he was peacefully asleep, his worrisome night forgotten. She lay as still as she could and wished she could telephone home. What if Trudy had left the kettle going and its liquid had boiled out? Trudy never left kettles going, but what if Joshu's cold had turned to croup? Parri had had it—terrible gasping spells that kept them up all night. It was too late to telephone and disturb them, so she promised herself to call first thing in the morning. Then she gently slipped Josh's arm back onto its own bed so she could turn and toss. She even watched the dawn creep across New York like a ghost—a dirty shabby ghost that envied its clean sister ghost in the country.

"Hey! Penny, wake up!" Josh shook her gently, when it seemed she had just closed her eyes. "It's almost nine-thirty," he said, "and we'll have to go out for our breakfast."

"Ugh." Penny sat up and blinked at the strange, disordered room. "What time is it?" she asked, not knowing he had told her.

"Late. Snap into it, baby."

"Ugh," she said again, and pulled herself to the side of the bed.

There was a new toothbrush in the bathroom cabinet, hygenically sealed in a glass tube and left there for any guest to whom Josh might lend the apartment, and she fumbled with the cap and silently blessed herself for her thoughtfulness. Cold water dashed over her face slapped sleep from her eyes, the sheet from her bed made a very good towel; but after a shower had brought her really awake, she stood in the center of the room like a white marshmallow and looked ruefully down at her pile of clothes. "I haven't a thing to wear," she said. "Look at my dress—it's a sight."

"What's wrong with it?" Josh had shaved and showered before he waked her and was fully dressed and shoving the beds back into place.

"It's wrinkled. And it's dirty, besides. It's a summer dress."

"Well, it is summer." He left the beds and gave the unlovely outfit a shake. "Not too bad," he decided. But Penny sat down in her sheet and stared at him.

"I can't meet strange people in a wrinkled cotton dress," she wailed. "I haven't any gloves."

"We'll buy you a pair in that shop by the drug store." It

was like old times, this hurrying to get off, and he patted the top of her head. "Anything else?" he asked. "Have you shoes?"

"Yes, I came in those." She picked up her black and white pumps that showed they had come on a bus and flinched when her bare feet stuck to the soles. No stockings. "That doesn't matter so much," she grunted. "It's stylish to go around New York with bare legs and no hat." And she looked up to ask, "Have we time to telephone home?"

"From the drug store. Is there anything I can hook or zip?"

"No, thanks." No one else had ever fed Joshu his breakfast. Even Parri couldn't remember when anyone else had. They might not eat. Joshu might not be *able* to eat. Babies had tonsilitis, sometimes. There was a story in the paper about one that had been rushed to the hospital, but not in time. He had choked to death on the way. Penny ran up the zipper on her wrinkled dress and hunted through her purse for a comb with most of its teeth out. Dog had eaten the teeth and she felt a wave of tenderness for him. Her lipstick, too, was a lopsided affair, and almost gone. It needed a lipstick brush and she hadn't one with her.

"All ready?" Josh asked, when she knew she looked like a fright—or exactly what she was, a woman who had come to New York without luggage. "Let's go."

She clung to him a little as they slid down in the elevator, just to the hem of his jacket which he couldn't notice. Her hunger had left her. Her stomach was now mad and refused the very thought of food. It turned over and crawled against her spine, pushing back, back, and making her heart pump harder to reach it. "You order for me," she said in the drug

store. "Just anything, while I telephone home." Her need
to hear Trudy's voice was urgent. She wanted to run to the
back of the store, to the booth, but Josh's eyes were on her.
They questioned her and searched for some sign of regret.
"I only want to check, Josh," she said quickly. "This is an
important day to me and I don't want to start it with one
single feeling of worry."

"All right, Pen, if you're sure that's all. You don't want
to back out? You can, you know."

"I don't." This was the first time in all the years she
had known Josh that she ever had wanted to hurry away
from him, that what he had to say was of less importance
than another person's voice; but she made herself stand
still. "Truly," she said. "I'm the happiest girl in town."

That satisfied him, or seemed to, for he nodded. "Run
along and give the blessings my love."

"Of course he doesn't know one's sick," she told herself,
tapping an impatient foot while she waited for Trudy's dear
voice. "He wouldn't be so casual if he did and he'd make me
go home." Then she gave a gasp and shouted over the wire,
"Oh, *Trudy!*" and promptly began to cry.

"It's just that I'm so relieved," she said, when she knew
everything was all right, that Joshu had eaten twice as much
breakfast as usual, after his hunger strike of yesterday, and
that Parri was out in the sunshine. "It was the longest night
I ever went through, but I'll be home as early as I can." She
had so little time that she pulled her purse open and dabbed
her tears with powder while she talked; and when she was
almost through but could have gone on listening forever,
Josh pushed open the door and said, "Your breakfast's
here."

"I'm coming. Trudy. . . ." With only a second, she slammed the door shut again. "Everything's all right," she said. "I'm going to be in the play and am kind of excited about it, so don't worry. Just carry on," she ended gallantly, and hung up.

CHAPTER VI

"DEAR ME, I feel like a novice," Penny said at the stage entrance. "What are you going to call me?" she asked, as Josh swung open the heavy door.

She clutched her new gloves with a death grip and he grinned at her. "What did I used to call you?" he asked.

"I don't remember."

"I said Miss Parrish. Sometimes I said Penny, or Miss Parrish, or whatever came into my head. I certainly didn't say Mrs. MacDonald."

"No, I guess you didn't." She stepped forward to peek into the dim interior. The usual doorman's wooden chair was empty. Dressing room keys hung in a neat row on the call board and there was no clutter of mail on the shelf below them. Light filtered through the gloom in dust rays, and suddenly, happily, it all looked and smelled familiar. "Dear me," she said, taking little sniffs, "I do remember this place."

"Then let's go in."

"Wait a minute." The door swung shut behind them and left them in gloom. "Don't you think you should go first and prepare them for me?" she asked. "After all, they left here last night thinking they had Neda and they come back to find me. It doesn't seem exactly kind to Neda for me to walk in as if I owned the place or as if we thought she wasn't good enough."

"I didn't expect to, darling. I thought I'd put you over on the fringe like a good little kibitzer while I made them a talk.

You see, we have to get out the original scripts now, and they'll have some re-learning to do."

"Oh, I hadn't thought of that."

"And we'll have to talk it over and go into it as a group. They'll be glad but I want them to understand it."

"I see."

Penny walked beside Josh like any wife accompanying her husband to his office. She could see dim light through cracks in the flats that walled a stage into a room; and when she went through a canvas door, it was as familiar as a homecoming. The stage manager had already set his scene— though goodness knew why, with things in the state they had been last night. People sat on wooden chairs that were placed about for sofas, even a fireplace and stairs, silent, waiting for their director, and wondering would they be jobless before ever they were paid. Something was wrong and they knew it. Mr. MacDonald had never been late before, and Miss Thayne's arrogant presence was missing.

Penny found a backless chair meant for a bookcase and sat down against a flat with trees painted on it. It was an odd room, like a forest turned inside out; for whatever could be found had been lashed together. The people in it were odd, too, and looked out of place. Mr. Cottingham was the only one she knew well, and he seemed much older than he had six years ago. Mrs. Forrester who, from Josh's description would play Anne's mother, was knitting; and Penny told herself that never would a cast be a cast without a knitter. Jervis Travers looked very handsome, just standing alone in pensive thought. The others, a young girl with great big eyes, a nervous juvenile, a middle-aged man, a spare woman who was certainly the starchy nurse off the stage as well as on, and a very small boy, sat stiffly on their chairs and waited. The little boy was the one who held Penny's attention. He was younger than she had thought he would be and looked much like Joshu might seven or eight years from now. "I wouldn't want my baby doing this," she said silently, and turned her gaze on Josh.

He was talking with Brooks and there was no doubt that Brooks looked happy. Even the dispirited actors felt it and perked up a little, all but Mrs. Forrester who was counting her stitches. Brooks pumped Josh's hand like a Jumping Jack before he loped over to Penny. Heads turned to follow him, and it took Josh's voice on the apron of the stage to bring them back.

"Give us more light, Steve," he called. "Lower the work-light." The queer room brightened and his face lighted up with it as he said, "Let me have your attention for a few minutes please, everyone. We've had to make a change in the cast. You all knew the play wasn't right as it was and I don't have to tell you, so we're going back to the original script. I know it will mean a lot more work for you with time as short as it is, with only eight days to go before we hit Philadelphia—but I think you'll bear me out when I say the thing didn't click. And I think, too, that you'd rather start over and do it the right way.

"We all prefer to take something sure—though nothing is ever sure in this business—than gamble on a play that looks bad from the start." He paused, waiting for their nods of approval. "Miss Thayne agrees with me. We talked it over last night." And how! he thought, plunging on. "She doesn't like the original Anne because she knows it doesn't suit her—but she does agree with me that the play's all wrong. So she offered to step out for a new Anne—and I think that's darn big of her—if I could find one. By luck and good fortune, I did." Josh stopped and grinned at them. Nothing could hold back his grin, although he did say seriously enough, "Sometimes the old saying holds true, that you can find a blue bird right in your own back yard—and I think I've caught us a dandy. My wife will play Anne." He stopped for the excited gasp his words brought, waited for applause that was much too loud for so few clapping hands to make, then said, "There she is, hiding in a corner. Come here, Penny."

Penny jumped. Like the others she had been listening to Josh. Her eyes had stung with tears at the way he said "my wife," and she was simply sitting there feeling proud of him. "Oh," she gasped.

"She's a little shy," Josh teased, going to meet her as she stood up. "She doesn't know much about acting, but she looks Anne to the life." Everyone laughed with him, and he added with his arm around her, "She asked me just now what I intend to call her, and I'll tell you so you won't be surprised. I'll call her Penny, Miss Parrish, stupe, dope, or darling, just as I do at home. And if you hear her fling a rousing "idiot" at me, just take it in your stride. We're family here. Now, come and meet her."

Penny was surrounded. Mr. Cottingham got there first by right of priority, Mrs. Forrester with blue wool spinning out behind her, and Penny stooped and kissed the little boy. He smelled of cold cream, the way actor children always seem to do, and she bent down and promised, "I'll bring my children in someday."

"We're so happy, Miss Parrish," the big-eyed girl said.

[108]

"I've always dreamed of playing with you, and it's the nicest thing that could happen to me."

"Thank you." Penny smiled and considered her title. Miss Parrish. It sounded all right.

Jervis Travers was the last to hold out his hand. He wanted to know what this change would mean to him and had waited until the others stepped back. "It's nice to have you with us, Miss Parrish," he said coldly. "Perhaps this play *does* need a star to carry it."

"Please don't feel that way." Penny looked up at him soberly. Her shyness was gone, her embarrassment over a wrinkled dress. She was no longer the contented girl of the country, but a woman who had come back to a type of work she understood. She seemed older, more confident; and when she spoke her words had the ring of great sincerity. "I realize what my coming into the play does to your part," she said. "Believe me, I'm sorry. Let's sit down together and discuss it."

The others walked carefully away and she waited while Jervis brought another broken chair, then sat beside him, her hands in her lap. "Mr. Travers," she said, "if I hadn't helped Josh out, we wouldn't have had a play. You know that as well as I do. And we both know it's a *woman's* play. It depends on the woman, and I'm only here because I'm needed. I don't want to rob you of anything, not your scenes or billing. Some of the padding will have to be taken out again, of course, because we'll go back to the original, but I don't expect to be the star or to be treated that way. I'm only part of the organization, as you all are."

"I appreciate that."

His voice was still stiff and she was thoughtful before she turned and looked straight at him. "No, you don't," she said, "and I can't blame you. You think you're being cheated."

"I'm glad you see it that way."

"But you aren't. You didn't feel so when you were engaged for the part, and you're exactly what you were then. You were satisfied, then."

"Yes, but since. . . ."

"I know." She broke into a soft laugh. "We're all alike. It's so easy to step up and so hard to drop back. But you won't, Mr. Travers, I promise you. Perhaps some of the padding can be left in. But, whether it can or not, the billing will read, "Penny Parrish and Jervis Travers," just as it was. The only change will be my name substituted for Neda Thayne's."

The stare he gave her was wary and unbelieving. "I'm afraid Mr. MacDonald will have something to say," he began, but she cut him off.

"Mr. MacDonald is my husband. He's so glad to have me," she said with complete candor, "that he'd put your name in electric lights if I told him to—so let's be friends. Will you do that for me, Mr. Travers?"

In spite of himself he was warmed. Penny looked at him so frankly and with such complete understanding of his position that he found himself saying, "I'd be glad to. I'm grateful to you, Miss Parrish, very grateful."

"Then suppose we hear what Josh has to say." She hoped she had made a friend, but if she had or if she hadn't, she knew she had side-stepped an enemy, so turned her attention to Josh and listened to him say:

"The first act is still the same so we'll work on that this

morning. By noon you'll have your old scripts back and we'll have to knock off while Miss Parrish learns her lines. Tomorrow, we'll work straight through with an hour off at six, for dinner. Penny?" He turned to his new star, said, "Brooks is making an appointment for your fittings at nine o'clock tomorrow morning. Okay?"

"Yes," she answered obediently; even while she wanted to ask, "How can I get in to town that early?"

She bit back her unspoken question and Josh answered it at one o'clock when he bustled her down the alley and said, "You'd better make out a list of clothes and all the stuff you'll need. I'll have John bring them in."

"Can't I even go home?" Penny was more tired than she ever had thought of being in the country. So much walking in her high heeled pumps without stockings had worn a blister on one toe, and she limped along beside him, pleading anxiously, "Couldn't I even drive out for a minute? I could learn my lines there."

"With time wasted going and coming and the kids running around? Don't be silly."

He marched on like the head of a parade, and by putting in extra hops she managed to keep up with him. She was back in a drug store, back on a stool at a counter; and even the loss of her freedom was nothing compared to the pain in her toe. With a sigh of relief she slipped off her shoe and tried to hide her bare foot under the folds of her dress. "It hurts," she said, knowing he didn't hear her. Then tried it a little louder. "My toe really hurts."

At that he looked down at her one visible leg and grinned. "What did you do with the other one, stork?" he asked.

"It's under me. Do you want to see the hole I've dug in it?"

"We'll bandage it up when we get home, but wait a minute." He went off and came back with a small box of Band Aids. "Gosh, but you're a lot of trouble," he grunted, crouching down and trying to complete an operation she insisted on keeping private. "How can I reach your toe when you've got it under your dress?"

"Oh, *here!*" Penny thrust out her foot for everyone to see. It didn't matter much, she reasoned, for no one in the rushing, pushing mob knew her. She wanted to go home and thought this was the time to say so—while she was Penny and he was still Josh. In no time at all her toe would be fixed and he would lapse into being the director again; so she said, "I like being in your show. But you'll have to admit that things have happened to me mighty fast. There isn't another woman in the world who wouldn't be allowed to tell her children good-by. Even a court of law lets them do that. And there isn't a woman either who can write down all the things she needs. Maybe a man can, you can, but a woman has to *see* her things."

"Meaning?" The bandage was in place and he gave it a firm adhering press that made her jerk.

"Ouch!" she yipped. "Meaning that, willy-nilly, *I'm* going home. I'll stay up all night and learn the lines I almost know already, but I'm going home first. I'm going to make one stop —then I'm going home."

"Where's the stop?" Josh climbed back on his stool, and she answered:

"Neda's. I won't feel right about taking that part till I talk to Neda. I won't stay long, though."

"All right." He reached for his sandwich but his hand

made a detour and patted her knee. "You'd better telephone first," he said, and promptly went off into his other world.

Penny got into a cab while Josh went to the garage for his car. She carefully rehearsed everything she would say to Neda; but when she stood in the square mirrored living room where so many of the two of them gazed at each other from the walls, it was like looking at a television show. "Do you mind if I sit down?" she asked. She would be below the mirrors that way.

"Of course not. You said you couldn't stay so I didn't suggest it."

Penny sank into a chair upholstered in leopard and gave the unfortunate animal a pitying pat before she looked at the other girl. Neda's face was quite composed but her eyes were puffed and had telltale rims that come from crying. "Neda," she said reluctantly, "I'm awfully sorry. I didn't want to be in the darned old play. I still don't, in a way, though I enjoyed it this morning."

"You're in."

"I know it. And I'll have to stay." She waited, watching the top come off of a crystal cigarette box, then leaned forward. "May I have one of those things?" she asked. "I never smoke, but what I have to say is awfully hard and I need something to fiddle with."

The box was passed without comment, and when she had put a cigarette in her mouth a lighter clicked and waited. "They're cork tipped," Neda said. "You have the wrong end in."

"Oh. Thanks." Penny inspected the white cylinder carefully before she clasped it between her lips and stuck it into the flame. It sparked as beautifully as the station wagon on a rampage and she hastily held it over an ash tray. "It's this way," she said, glad to be so busy. "The whole mess was my fault from the very beginning. You didn't have a Chinaman's chance in that part because Josh was never going to see any-one in it, but me. He took it for me and he was trying to turn you into me. He didn't know it, but he was. *I* knew it. I tried to tell myself I didn't, but I'm sure I knew. I kept butting in that first week end out at our house because I was sort of hoping you'd get the hang of the thing." She paused, tap-ping her cigarette against glass, and when there was no an-swer, looked up. "Don't you believe me?" she asked.

"Yes."

"Then it all boils down to this: Josh is my husband and I love him. I could have told him last night what I'm telling you now, and urged him to keep on trying. Perhaps your Anne would have turned out better than mine, but we'll never know, because he wouldn't have been satisfied with it. He comes first with me, Neda, so I had to step in and help him."

"Right you are." Neda ground out her cigarette that was much farther smoked than Penny's. "As long as you think you're right, you're right," she said flatly.

"I don't think it. I just had to do what seemed best. This seemed to be it and I hoped you'd understand."

"Oh, I do." The words were spoiled by a shrug, and Penny stood up. The conversation was over. It had ended like the cigarettes in their glass trays, in ashes. "I'm terribly sorry," she said with disappointed dignity. "Some actress would have had to step into your part and I'm only sorry I was the one. That's what I came to tell you." She walked slowly to-ward the door, then stopped and faced all the reflected Pennys without being conscious of them. "There's just one more thing I want to add," she said. "Not as Josh's wife or to justify myself, but because I mean it. You're a darn good actress, Neda. Smart, scintillating, breezy and brittle. Foolish sentimental little Anne wouldn't have helped your career, she'd have done you more harm than good. Think about that and go out and land the lead in Craig Dalton's new comedy. It's a honey. Josh will speak to him tomorrow about you." Neda still sat in silence, so she ended, "Good-by. Please come out and see us soon," and let herself out.

"Zowie, but this has been a day!" she told Josh, hopping into the coupé and slamming the door so he could make the light before it changed. "I got by with Jervis Travers but I failed with Neda. She's mad."

"Did you think she wouldn't be? At both of us? She'll hate me forever."

"That's nice." Penny looked pleased and too knowing as she turned and grinned at him. "I'd rather she'd be mad over losing *you* than losing the part—and she is. I have you and she couldn't get you. Watch out for that truck."

His hand had been fumbling around on the seat and it now came up with the familiar blue-jacketed play. "Get started," he ordered. "I'll do the driving."

"Oh, me." She flattened out the pages, held the book against her chest, and said above it, "I have two more reminders for you to write in your little black book. One of them is—now don't yelp or I won't come back from the country—one of them is that Jervis Travers' name gets billed along with mine." The yelp was coming and her hand flew to cover his mouth. "The other one," she went on into his inarticulate protest, "is that, tomorrow morning, while I

have my darned old dresses made, you hump yourself straight
down to Craig Dalton's office and put out the best pep talk
you ever made, for Neda. Will you do those things?"

"Ur-r-rg." Josh pulled her hand away and got her face
in his vision instead.

"Will you?" she demanded. "I couldn't sleep a wink, ever
again, if you don't. Not even in my beautiful retirement,
which I shall settle into *immediately* if you say no."

"You'd be a widow."

"No, I wouldn't. You're a good kind father and you
wouldn't let your children suffer for your mistakes. You'd
come out. But will you do it?"

"I'll try to fix it for Neda—but, now about Travers. . . ."

"Thank you, darling. I'll learn my lines now."

Penny sat back and began to work. She worked so hard
that her mind rarely flashed to the joyful fact that she was
headed toward home. But from the second they turned off
the highway, her heart was far out ahead of the car; and
when her very own gravel crunched under the tires, she flung
open the door and was ready to jump.

Joshu was in his play pen under the tree and he was the
most beautiful baby she had ever seen. When Parri's laugh
rang out from behind the house, she snatched him up and
ran toward it. She was dizzy with joy when she had the
two of them clutched to her and sat down on the grass to
enjoy it.

"Mummie, you hurt," Parri complained, pushing away.
"You're funny. Did you have a nice time?"

"I was lonesome." Joshu had discovered her eyes and was
gouging one out, and she squinted up through the other one
as Parri flew high into the air and up to Josh's shoulders.

"I was so lonely I had to come back," she said, rolling the baby over and kissing him. "Did you miss me?"

"We had a party." Parri proclaimed the happy news from her high perch and added urgently, "If you go right back to town with Daddy, we can have a party every day. Trudy said so. Just me and Joshu and Trudy. When Davy comes home we'll invite him."

"My, my, how they suffered," Josh said, swinging Parri through the air by her feet, down and up again, and catching her neatly, with his hands around her waist. "Poor kids."

"Quiet, you." Penny wrinkled up her nose, stuffed Joshu into his arms, too, and went off to check her establishment.

"Well, I've done it, Trudy," she said, after she had paid her respects to Minna, first, as befitted the cook, and cornering Trudy on the side porch. "Do you think you can manage? I won't be home for a week. Josh says I can't come out before we go to Philadelphia, so you'll have to pack and be ready."

"Law, Miss Penny, *we* ain't goin', is we?"

"Of course, you are. And now about grocery money and getting together all the things I have to take back." Penny rattled on at a brisk pace, then suddenly stopped. "I'm not happy," she said.

"Oh, but you is, child."

"Not like I was out here in the sunshine. I'm excited—but I'm not happy. I'm strung up on wires, and most of the time I'm not even me. I'm *vedy vedy* intelligent, which I'm not. Lots of times this morning I didn't know exactly who I was, Anne, Miss Parrish, or Penny MacDonald. It's confusing. And people in town dislike one another. They fight and are jealous."

She got up abruptly and went inside. She went straight

to the living room and took photographs of her family from their familiar places. She chose one of her father in uniform, in boots and breeches and a cocky overseas cap; a tinted one of her mother that had a smile and soft brown eyes; Bobby in bathing trunks; and little Tippy in the white dress she had worn on her sixteenth birthday. "There," she said. "Perhaps it won't be so bad if I have you all with me and scatter my own two children all over the place."

The rest of her packing was easy. She whirled through it, leaving her dresses on hangers, and was back on the porch by the time the children's supper was ready. "This is a party, too," she said, sitting down between them. "It's a very *special* one for me." And she called to Minna, "If Dog hasn't eaten we'd like to invite him."

It was over all too soon; baths, prayers, and goodnight kisses. It was dark again, just as it had been last night, and time to go back to the new world she had set out to find.

This new world was busy, hectic, once familiar but now strange. Josh was a tyrant. He worked her early and late and until she was ready to drop. The costumes Kartrel designed didn't suit him. The *peignoirs* didn't trail enough, the nightgowns needed zippers to make them fit, he wanted her in red for the last act. "Not an imitation red," he yelled, pushing away the bolts of cloth, "a flaming *fireman's* red!" And they started all over.

Penny stood for hours while people pinched and pinned and crawled around her. A nightgown, she had always thought, was a thing you pulled over your head and tied with a belt. A red wool dress was what you bought in a store, twisted around a bit to see, said, "It's nice, I'll take it." The pastel robes he chose made her ashamed for the neat models she had taken to the hospital when the children were born.

She was tired most of the time. She crawled into bed tired and got up the same way. Concentration over the exact number of ounces to go into a baby's formula was simple compared to computing the exact number of leko spots needed for sunshine; and because she lived with the producing end as well as the acting, she dreamed of flats, ex-ray borders, teasers and props.

Josh was completely happy and completely mad through it all. He did inquire for his children's health when she telephoned them, but she was sure he didn't hear what she answered. His unruly hair went in all the wrong directions and the only tie he had thought to bring with him was yanked into a string.

"Living here with you is positively indecent," she said one morning, plopping his bacon and eggs before him. "You never even know I'm here." His eyes stayed glued to a mass of notes before him and she bent over. "Don't you remember me?" she asked.

He lifted his head and regarded her vaguely. "I seem to," he said. "Are you the cook?"

"I'm the lady who lives here."

"Ah, yes, now I know." He laid his pencil down with a happy smile. "You're the one who wears the pink silk nightgown and the traily pink robe with lace ruffles, aren't you?"

Penny stalked back to her pantry-kitchen and called over her shoulder, "That's Anne. I'm the cute one."

"Do tell." He rested his elbows on the table and watched her strike a tabloid posé, the tip of her shoe just touching the floor, knee bent, dress pulled up to show her leg. "I wonder how I've missed seeing you around," he said. "You're a honey. Could I make a date with you sometime?"

"Tonight." She floated back with the toast, swayed and ran a hand under his chin, then whisked away.

"Have you been with me long?" he asked.

"For almost a week. I was a pretty young thing when you married me." Penny got her own plate and sat down opposite him at the wobbly gateleg table. She was dressed for work as he was, with one of Trudy's voluminous aprons over her navy blue dress, and she finished her sentence with a large, round sigh. "Even pretending has lost its kick," she said. "I pretend all day, now."

"You always did. The only difference is, you're going to be paid for it." He decided he had entertained her long enough and went back to his notes, so she was left to look grumpily around the room and silently tell her family, "See how he treats me? You wouldn't believe it if you couldn't see for yourselves." Her mother's smile remained fixed and her father stayed so pleasantly content that she said aloud, "Oh, bosh!" And Josh looked up.

"Did you speak to me again?" he asked, and she giggled.

"Nope, one letter was wrong. But I might have said that it's time to go to work. *I'm* the one who says it," she reminded, sunny again. "*I'm* the eager beaver who wants to be off and away."

But at last the week was over. Even the long night of dress rehearsal ended. Nothing went right. Telephones rang instead of doorbells, or didn't ring at all; props were wrong, lights were wrong, chairs were too big to walk around with the grace rehearsed; actors froze on their cues; and there was so much starting, stopping, and waiting for repairs that it was almost five o'clock before Penny and Josh got back to the apartment that had at last begun to seem like home.

Josh went into the dark foyer with his hand out for the light switch and fell over a line of luggage. "Good Lord, what's this?" he groaned, before Penny turned on the light and he found out. "Are you taking all *that?*" he asked.

"Umhum." She ran her finger along, counting the pieces, and nodded. "It's all here," she said. "But I don't think we'll need the little refrigerator."

"What little refrigerator?"

"The one we keep baby food in when we travel. It's such a short trip that. . . ."

"What has baby food got to do with it?" he asked. He thought he knew, hoped he didn't, but was sure he did when she answered:

"I'm taking a lot of cans with me. We may not be able to get the right things in a hotel so I told Trudy to pack a box, but I didn't tell her. . . ."

"Do you mean *Joshu's* going with us?"

"Oh, yes, and Parri. Trudy, too."

"Ye gods!" He sat down and stared at her. "Listen, Pen," he said. "This isn't a family jaunt. We're going off on business. You can't fool with the kids."

"I can kiss them sometimes. I never went off and left them before. I simply couldn't keep my mind on my acting," she explained, "if I didn't know how they were getting along."

"You've done it here."

"Well," Penny sat down, too, and murmured apologetically, "I know I did. But you see, Brooks telephoned home for me every three hours and reported. He couldn't do that down there."

Her eyes were big and troubled as they looked into his and Josh tried not to seem so hard or even so stunned. "You do take the cake," he growled. "What are you planning to do with them in Philadelphia? I suppose you and Brooks have worked that out."

"Yes, but not Brooks. I called up myself and made a reservation. I thought you'd be pleased about it but I didn't want to bother you, so I had your manager check on it for me. I got them a sitting room and two bedrooms and bath. That's so they won't have to be downstairs at all," she said, unsure now. "They can stay in the drawing room on the train. They won't be any trouble."

She spoke so hesitantly and looked so sure he detested his children that Josh was suddenly ashamed. "Poor, funny, little kid," he said, knowing he should be firm and leave all their excess baggage behind, but giving in. He knew, too, that one had to keep an actress calm before an opening night and avert every crisis. He would have walked on his hands to soothe her nerves, so he tried to sound hearty and do the thing he found much harder. "Fine," he said, hoping she wouldn't notice the way his voice croaked, and trying to cover it up with a yawn. "How did we get the bags and boxes up here?"

"John brought them. He'll bring the rest with the children, tomorrow."

That was too much. His nerves were jangled, too, and he couldn't face a train ride with a pair of happy little people. "No good," he said grimly, and made the mistake of suggesting, "You and I are taking the two o'clock and going straight to the theater. I think we'd better have Trudy come later with the kids and let Brooks or somebody meet them. We don't open until the following night, you know, and after we've ironed out some rough spots, you can have all evening with them."

"We won't be through before midnight." Penny doubled over and hid her face on her knees. Then she did exactly what Josh had tried to prevent. She burst into tears.

He knew she wept from exhaustion and it sent him running for her nightgown. The gown was a puffed sleeve affair, simple enough to get on her, except that he tried to pull down the beds at the same time. He struggled with both, and when he wasn't busy at other things, like spilling a bottle of milk all over the vestibule floor, dabbed at her tears.

The tears flowed in an endless stream and even Penny couldn't stop them. "I'm so blank," she wept. "I can't remember my lines. Oh, Josh, I can't remember *my lines!*"

"You will in the morning." He carried her to the bed and brought the milk. "Here, darling," he soothed, holding her up. "Drink this."

"I—can't . . . I'll choke."

"No, you won't. Wait a minute." He found a bottle of cognac and poured a generous splash into the milk. "This'll do the trick," he said, in spite of her shudder. "Drink it down."

Penny's teeth chattered against the glass and he took it from her shaking hands and held it steady. "Nerves," he said calmly. "Blasted things—but they happen sometimes. You've done as much in a week as it took the rest of us four to do. Lie down, now."

She went back with a plop and rolled over, flat on her face. Her sobs were muffled by the pillow and they gradually lessened to wavering hiccoughing breaths. Her trembling stopped as Josh sat on the bed beside her, gently running his hand up and down her spine, up and down, with soothing rhythm. "I'm trying," she whispered at last. "I'm not thinking—just trying."

" 'Atta girl."

"Please come to bed. You're so tired. . . ."

"In a minute." His hand continued its even stroke, long after his shoulder ached with steady pain and she lay quiet. When he was quite sure she was asleep, he eased himself to his feet and found his pajamas. Then he turned out the light and bent over to kiss her tumbled hair.

His own bed welcomed him, and it was almost noon before he remembered her again. He only did it then because the telephone was screaming above the chatter of small happy voices in the hall.

Penny was sitting straight up. "They're here!" she cried, and he hadn't seen her dash out of bed so fast since they had left the country. She looked just as she used to when she had overslept Joshu's bottle, and she scooted across the room in her bare feet.

The telephone gave another angry screech and he reached out for it. "Yeah, Brooks, we're up," he said, yawning and rumpling his hair. "Yeah, we'll be at the station on time." Something starchy climbed on his chest and he added, "All of us," before he hung up and kissed Parri.

CHAPTER VII

Josh sat in the front of the parlor car, talking with Brooks and his manager. He needed Penny's opinion on one or two matters but, given the choice, would have put his head in a lion's cage rather than open the drawing room door. Some sort of exciting game was going on and little Nicky Carter was in there, too. The small actor had left his mother reluctantly, marching along the aisle ahead of Penny like a bored midget in long pants, but now he was shouting with the rest of them.

The meeting of the company at the train gate had been something to behold: Quiet and controlled until the MacDonald contingent arrived, and from then on like an Elk's picnic on the loose. The crew had gone ahead with the scenery: the electrician, the carpenter, property man, and the assistant stage director, but they had left behind the raucus old woman whom Penny always used for her theater maid. Ma Harkins was advancing in years but she still wore the same red wig that made her look like an imitation Sarah Bernhardt, falling apart. Penny laughed with her, obeyed her and loved her; for Ma was her luck piece and had been ever since she had shared her with two other girls in her first Broadway play. Ma's billowing body had detached itself from the quiet gathering and had met them in a head-on collision and with its fog horn blowing. Now it took up most of a seat in the drawing room, and her happy commands boomed through the solid door like a good top sergeant's. Josh liked her but stayed clear in moments of crisis.

Brooks lounged against the swaying wall of the car and Mr. Williams, the manager and a fussy little man who always walked with his stomach preceding him, sat on the edge of his lounge chair, notebook on his pin-striped knee, his Knight Templar charm swinging from a gold watch chain across his vest. The rest of the company read or dozed, and enjoyed an hour's rest and relaxation.

"Lord, I've got to talk to Travers," Josh said, running a hand through his black hair that couldn't stay smooth. "I hate to, but I only have a few minutes left. What's he doing?"

"Reading." Brooks glanced along the car and Josh stood up.

"Here I go," he said, and walked back down the aisle.

Jervis Travers was looking at printed words but he felt Josh coming; and when the heavy green chair in front of him swung around, he raised his head. "We're on our way," Josh said, sitting down and facing him. "Sink or swim, success or failure, tomorrow night's the night. We'll know then if we're any good, or not." He reached into his jacket pocket and took out the regulation theater program. "Williams brought this back from a printer in Philly," he said, opening it and holding it a moment before he passed it across. "I want you to see it, Jervis. It's the best I could do." The actor's eyes stayed lifted above the page, and he went on, "I know what Penny wanted, but we couldn't quite make it. She's a drawing card and we need it. Any show, no matter how good it is, needs someone to pull in the people. Penny pulls them in."

Jervis looked down at the opened page. It held exactly what he had expected to see. *"Joshua MacDonald presents*

. . ." with Penny Parrish in capital letters, "*PENNY PARRISH.*" And underneath, an insignificant "*in,*" then capitals again, "*ONE STEP TO HEAVEN. A play by Frederick Lampson.*"

The part to follow was what interested him; and he found another small word, a small but important "*with,*" and his own name beneath it. His letters were almost as large as Penny's, not quite but almost, and he dwelt on them for some seconds before he nodded. "It's okay, Josh," he said. "I know it's the best you could do."

"Will you tell Penny that? She's not going to like it."

"I'll tell her." Jervis gave the program back. "She's a swell girl and I'd rather work with her than be co-billed with Neda," he said. "I think I'll get more out of it in the end and have a chance for a longer run."

"Good." Josh stuffed the folder back into his pocket and got up. "Thanks, fellow," he said, resting his hand on Jervis' shoulder. "I'm grateful." Then he squared his shoulders and looked out at the streets and rows of apartment houses sliding by. "We're almost in," he sighed, "and, oh, dear Lord, how I dread it."

The drawing room door opened and little Nicky rushed out. He looked less like a precocious juvenile and more like a little boy returning from a birthday party, his hands filled with favors. Crayons spilled from a box as he ran along the aisle, and bored passengers turned their heads and wondered who all the people were who knew each other so well. A woman asked, "Did you have a good time, Nicky?" and the two men accompanied the porter in and out of the drawing room, carrying a seemingly endless number of bags.

"Now, this is the way it's going to be," Josh said firmly,

after he had piloted his family through the station and had them safely on the pavement of the taxi entrance. "Brooks will take Trudy and the kids to the hotel, and Penny, you're coming with me." He held Joshu in the crook of one arm and leaned away from the fond mother who was trying to push back the baby's small white beret so strangers could see some of what little hair he had. "Let him alone. And give Parri to Trudy."

Trudy had been left with nothing to carry but the little case that held toys and Joshu's extra underpants, and she reached down for a small white glove that was willing to be held by anyone. Parri was being a good little girl. She had no idea what all this was about, so stayed a good little girl while she found out; but Joshu was tired of it all. When Trudy seated herself in the taxi and reached out to take him, he threw back his head and grew stiff. His face turned red and his screams could be heard for a block.

"I'd better go with him," Penny said anxiously, putting a foot in the cab door; but Josh pulled her back.

"He'll calm down. He always does, as soon as we're out of sight," he told her, thinking that Joshu really was a pitiful sight, squatting on Trudy's lap with his arms held out. "We aren't abandoning him forever, you know."

"But we look like it. People are staring at us and we look like it. If Parri starts to cry. . . ."

Parri waved. She never had ridden in such a funny car and she waved dutifully at Trudy's bidding. " 'By, Mummy, 'by, Daddy," she piped, her face as round and shining as the doll's she clutched. And she sat down only when Brooks crawled in and the cab lurched off.

"Now you see?" Josh said, praying she would. "They're

going to be fine. They'll have a nap and be ready to play by the time you get to the hotel."

"They'll be in bed and up again, having their breakfast." This was no way to begin a business trip, even she knew it; and she tried to dismiss the taxi cab with its precious load. "All right," she said, "let's go. You were sweet to let me bring them with me, so I'll carry on. I will, Josh, truly," she promised. "I wish I didn't love them so much," she sighed, stepping into another waiting cab, "or else that I could be like a man and have neat pigeonholes in my heart. Business in this slot, family in the next one. I wonder if women will ever be able to do it?"

"Probably, after they've been in business as long as men have. They're still rather new at it."

"I know." Penny looked out at the buildings, the restaurants, the bars, where men and women alike, hurried in and out. "Gone are the lace curtain days," she said thoughtfully. "I remember my grandmother telling us that every evening Grandfather would say, as regularly as clockwork, 'Well, Mabel, I think I'll just run down to the cigar store for an hour or so while you put the children to bed.' "

"Did she mind?"

"I don't know. She told it in defense of Dad when he tried it once. He called upstairs that he thought he'd drive over to the Officers Club, and Mums shouted down, 'Dave Parrish, you come up here and help me so I can go, too.' Grandmother clicked and clucked and said, 'Why, Marjorie!' But he waited. They went off looking awfully cute," Penny remembered. "Mums had on one of those long-wasted, short-skirted dresses and fuzzy bobbed hair. Sometimes I thought she looked more like a little girl than a mother."

"Perhaps ours will feel that way about us," he answered, "if we're always dashing in and out, full of plans. Don't you think it's better, Penny?"

"Yes, I do. I think it's harder, but it's better. I think, too, that I should have left the children at home and come off with you, alone. Just dismissed them from my mind and thought of you." A street car clanged beside them, she saw her name spelled with unlighted electric bulbs above the theater marquee, and sighed. "I'm trying, Josh," she said soberly. "It's a lesson that's awfully hard for me to learn, but the more I work at it the better I'll do. Women have a whale of a row to hoe."

"Anyway you take it." He grinned at her, and added, waiting for the cab to stop, "Either in your day or your grandmother's."

"But I'm glad I am one. I'd rather worry and be a mother than just a father," she laughed, stepping out beside him. Then she remembered what she had seen in lights, and looked at the billboards flanking the theater's entrance. "Josh MacDonald!" she cried. "You promised!"

"I did the best I could," he said, paying the fare and following her when she walked over to one of the large framed placards and stood reading it. "Jervis is satisfied. He thinks his name is big enough."

"But you prom. . . ." Penny shook her head and closed her lips.

"That's another lesson a woman has to learn, Pen," he said. "Business is business, and it doesn't run on sentiment. Perhaps that's one reason why a woman may never make a good President, and few of them ever rise to be a top executive. They aren't ruthless enough. They won't climb up on the shoulders of the little people. They won't hire and fire cold-bloodedly because their sentiment mixes in; and the average woman isn't good at politics, at conceding, dickering, compromising, in order to win a point."

"Thank goodness." She turned away and walked beside him down the theater alley. "There am I in electric lights," she said. "Big me. And where are Neda and Jervis?"

"In a spot they've earned," he answered equably. "You have a better mousetrap."

"I don't believe it." She started through the door he held open, but he stopped her.

"Neda had a chance at the part, didn't she?" he asked, and went on at her mute nod, "she muffed it. She wasn't right for it. It's just the same in every business, Pen. A brick mason may be tops but he can't lay hardwood flooring. Neda's no gal for subtle comedy; she has to slam it in with a wallop. Jervis will never be more than one of the bigger little people. You might just as well make up your mind that life is the way it is and stop worrying about it. Take what you have and be glad."

"Thank you, darling." She made him a bow and he let her pass. And all during the trying rehearsal, she watched him work like a machine and wondered what she ever had done to deserve him. She even asked Ma.

"Well," Ma answered, unpacking the big wardrobe trunk and hanging Penny's costumes on hangers before she pressed them, "I've always thought *he* was the one who oughta feel that way about you. I guess he does. Josh is a pretty sensible fellah." She almost filled the small dressing room, in her big flat shoes and flying red hair. She would be the perfect maid tomorrow. The dangling bracelets would be laid away, she would have a tight red knob on the back of her head and a starched dress stretched over her ample body; but today she was a lady who traveled first class and had dressed herself for the part. She jingled and jangled around while Penny rested and watched her.

"You're nice, Ma," she said, lazily unpacking the tin make-up box on her dressing table shelf, laying out a jar of cold cream and sticks of grease paint, rouge and eyebrow pencils. "I can't see why I don't get excited and nervous like everyone else. I feel so cold and calm inside."

"You will. By tomorrow night, you'll be havin' the jitters along with the rest of them. Just wait—you'll get 'em."

"Oh, gosh, I hope so."

Penny answered fervently, for to go to pieces on an opening night is part of the acting profession. Actors work themselves into a frenzy comparable to a saddle class in a horse show. Gaited horses are "waked up" in the privacy of their stalls, whipped, tuned to the snapping point, and released into the ring like a chorus of ballet dancers. Actors torture themselves. They pace or cry, according to their sex, thumb frantically through their scripts for a forgotten line, plead with their minds, their hands and feet, to guide them, then prance out as the horses do, brilliant and well-trained.

Penny decided she was the exception to prove the rule. She had a lump in her chest. It was such a large lump that no emotion squeezed past it. She even knew her lines. She had said them all day while she played with the children, silently under their racket, and in a monotonous murmur when she lay down for a nap. She was hungry, too, and enjoyed the frugal meal Josh had sent up. Her make-up went on smoothly, applied with a steady hand, and she could stand quite still while Ma dressed her.

"Nuts," she complained, leaning over to watch Ma adjust the folds of her long satin nightgown which was as lovely as a wedding dress. "I'm too calm."

A call boy knocked on the door, said, "Five minutes, Miss Parrish. Five minutes. Curtain in five minutes"—and it happened. She went to pieces like an undersized atom bomb.

"Ma!" she gulped wildly. "Look on side one and see what I say when he says . . . no, I'll do it myself. Where's my script? It was here! It. . . ." She rummaged along the make-up shelf and knocked off her mirror. "Oh, where *is* it?" she wailed, "I can't go on till I find it. Run ask the prompter . . . no, wait. Oh, dear heaven, I think I'm going to be sick."

"Here's your bed jacket and we still have to put your robe on top." Ma held out a flimsy affair and helped one of Penny's flaccid arms into the sleeve. "There we are," she soothed, as if talking to a child. "Let's watch out for your hair. Now, the robe."

Penny stood with her eyes shut. "I don't know the line," she repeated. "I'll never remember it. Where's Josh?"

"Where he ought to be, I suppose; keeping that useless author out of the way. Try to hold still."

"I can't." Penny shook from her head to her pink satin mules. "Oh, help me, Ma," she groaned. "Can't you think of the line?"

"I've never heard it." Ma Harkins went on dutifully snapping a snap and tying a sash while Penny rang her hands. "You're ready," she said, "and it's time to go." She opened the door and helped a dazed patient into a wheel chair that waited in the corridor, did more arranging of folds, and rolled her toward the wings.

Mr. Cottingham was marching up and down. He had been on and off, and felt fine. "Wonderful audience," he commented happily. "Gave quite a hand at my exit."

Penny sat in a trance. Life had fled from her hands. They lay limply in her lap and Ma reached down to put them on the rubber-tired wheels. "It's time now, dearie," she whispered. "On you go, now."

Something in Penny heard her. It heard someone on the stage say, "I know my wife will be glad to see you, Doctor," and it started her wheels. She was moving. She rolled straight into a room and a bright patch of sunshine, and she remembered the line. The line was there, waiting to be said when the applause ceased; and it came out with a breathless catch when she looked past her husband at the man she loved. "Good afternoon, Doctor," was all it was.

The play was on, the play was over. The cast had bowed and bowed and bowed. Even the author had bowed. Penny's smile was happy, for Philadelphia loved her. They loved her so much they hated to let her go, even after Brooks had signaled for house lights. "Okay, once more," he called, and the curtain slid up again with the cast skittering into their places. When it finally dropped and stayed there, Penny went back to what she had been doing, which was letting Josh hug her.

"Do you think it's a hit?" she asked. And he answered:

"How do I know? We'll have to wait for the papers. The crowd liked it at any rate, so it can't be *too* bad. Are you hungry?"

"I'm starved."

"Then suppose we wait up and read about ourselves? I've planned an after-the-show party for New York, but not here. Anybody who wants to go back to the hotel with us can tag along."

All the cast went. All but the small Nicky who was hustled off to bed. They sat in a stuffy night club with the morning editions spread out on a long table, hunched over, each searching for praise of himself, hoping for more, but satisfied.

"Well, I guess we're okay," Josh decided at last. "The notices are good. No great blast about *One Step to Heaven* being the show of the year or winning the Pulitzer Prize, but good enough to take us into New York." His voice held neither satisfaction nor disappointment, was simply matter-of-fact, and Penny leaned across to him.

"You *are* pleased, aren't you?" she asked anxiously.

"Sure. One hurdle is behind us and we can go on. I'm not all atingle like Fritz there. Mr. Frederick Lampson thinks the critics should rave about him and forget the rest of you. He doesn't like it because the boys have pointed out a couple of weak spots that we'll have to repair while we're here. I should have seen them myself, but didn't. Suppose we set a rehearsal for two o'clock and call off Penny's broadcast. She won't have time to make it."

It was the first Penny had heard about being on the air and she was glad to nod with the others. "Two o'clock," she yawned, watching Josh gather up their set of papers and signal for the check. "All I want to do now, is crawl into bed. I never did realize what a wonderful invention the box spring is, and, believe me, I'm planning to get my money out of the one I have here."

But, when she left Philadelphia four days later, she felt the hotel still owed her half of the bill Josh paid; not for the childrens' suite, for they had made constant happy use of it, but for the fine sitting room that was filled with baskets and vases of flowers, wilting and dying unseen, their cards carefully saved by Trudy, and the comfortable bedroom.

Even going back to New York offered no rest, for she told the children good-by at the apartment house door and watched them drive off with John. Then she unpacked her clothes and Josh's, decided what looked wearable and what must go to the cleaners—and put on her hat and coat again.

"Second lap of the same rat race," she said to Josh on opening night, watching him read a letter at her make-up shelf while Ma dressed her. "Haven't you anything *else* to do?"

"Plenty." He knew she was nervous but he looked up and grinned. "Know your lines?" he asked.

"Not one. If you'd only go *away!*" Her whole body tensed in a shudder and Ma walked over to throw open the door.

"Out, you!" she ordered. "You know better than to sit in here and upset her. Go on!"

Josh took his time about rising. He kissed Penny's perspiring cheek carefully and without disturbing her powder, and whispered, "You're swell, darling, so stop worrying. There's not a darned thing to worry about. Take it easy." Then he folded his letter and went out.

The letter was from David and it worried him more than Penny's nervousness. It worried him along with it, for he knew that at any minute she might ask, "Have David and Carrol come? Have you seen them?" And they weren't coming.

"Carrol's sick," David had written, and sent the note in by special messenger. *"Don't know exactly what it is—nervous*

*crack-up or something. I know how busy you are, but would
appreciate it if you could come out when the play gets running. You'll have to think up some sort of story for Pen when
we don't show for your party—the kids, I suppose. Don't let
her worry. Good luck, boy, I'm rooting for you."*

The whole letter sounded strangely unlike David, terse and
disconnected. Josh stuck it in his pocket and decided to telephone him from the box office when the play got under way.
At the moment, there were a dozen things to claim his attention. He settled several of them, saw the prompter in his place
in the wings, gave the nervous Brooks a steadying pat, and
let himself into the theater through a door behind a row of
boxes, just as the house lights dimmed.

The audience had settled into quiet. Women were taking
off their hats and smoothing their hair; programs whispered
little rustling noises as they were folded and laid on laps; a
late couple squeezed through to middle seats on the center
aisle. It was curtain time.

Josh stood with his eyes on the stage. The bright gay set
Ray Belcher had designed brought a burst of applause. Old
Cottingham got off to a fine start, and the clapping for Jervis
should have satisfied even him. The others played to interested silence. It was time for the line Josh waited to hear, and
he listened to a dapper, smug roué say boredly, "I'm sure my
wife will be glad to see you, Doctor."

A flurry of anticipation passed along the rows like a rip-
pling breeze. Spectators sat a little forward as the actors
turned to watch the door; then the theater was rocked by applause. Josh stared at the stage with the others. He felt his
throat tighten, his jaw muscles tense. My *wife,* he thought.
My wonderful wife.

THE RELUCTANT HEART

For a moment Penny in her wheel chair was a blur. She was an indistinct pink blur to him until he reached up and rubbed his tired eyes. His fingers came away suspiciously moist and he gave a deep sigh of triumph. My wife, he thought again, and couldn't control a proud grin.

It was hard to leave her and make his way to the box office, but he walked up the dark aisle past the standees along the rail at the back, and through a door, without looking behind him. There was a line of advance-sale buyers before the window and he said to the man who was selling to it, "All right if I use the phone, Joe?"

"Sure. How's it going?"

"Okay." Josh picked up the receiver that had been taken from its cradle and laid on a desk, then changed his mind. This place was too public for whatever David had to tell him, and he said, "I guess I'll go in the office."

"Williams and Mather are counting receipts in there."

"Oh." It seemed a long time before he heard the telephone ringing at Gladstone, and longer still before David's voice answered. "Hello, Dave," he said. "I called you as soon as I could. How's Carrol?"

"Wait a minute." He could hear David leave the telephone and close a door; then he came back. "I don't know," he answered. "The doctor gave her something to put her to sleep. It hasn't worked, but she's quiet."

"What happened?"

"Lord, Josh, I don't know that, either. Davy's out of his braces, you know; and Carrol's been so calm through the whole thing, until it was all over, that the doctor said it was nervous shock and reaction. I didn't know anything was wrong till today, but it seems she's been having what she describes as spells of panic—the feeling that she'd have to get up and run. It would start with a fluttery quiver in her chest, she said; even when she was having a good time or talking to people. I remember now that for the last week or so she's been asking me to read aloud or talk to her and hold her hand. I thought she gripped too hard but she didn't say anything and I didn't either. Today she passed out and we had a heck of a time bringing her to."

"Is she. . . ."

"She's perfectly rational, if that's what you mean," David answered, forestalling the question. "The thing to do is keep her relaxed so the fluttery feelings won't start. She sniffs ammonia when they do and hangs on to someone. I've got a nurse. It isn't a critical thing, Josh," he went on, "and no need for you or Pen to rush out, but I had to tell you. I feel awfully alone out here and have been wondering if I ought to cable for Mums. I don't think there's any danger. . . ." His voice trailed off into a sigh, and Josh said quickly:

"We'll be out tomorrow. We can make it. Pen can skip the party and we'll be out early. We'll talk it all over then, Dave."

"All right. I. . . . Sorry, but I'll have to go." The receiver clicked.

Josh stood holding the silent telephone a moment, then gently laid it down and asked, "Still want it off the hook, Joe?"

"Yeah. I can't take any calls."

He walked back slowly. The first act was over and people were pouring out through the lobby to stretch their legs and smoke. He scarcely heard their praise, the excited babble or discussions, the repeated word, "hit." Carrol was the quiet one, serene and quiet. She had been a tower of strength when little Davy was taken to the hospital. Perhaps she *had* been afraid to leave her younger child at home when she went to Warm Springs; to leave him down at the beach when Davy's braces had to be changed. If so, she had been afraid quietly and silently, without complaint. Then the happy end had come and all her nerves had let go. Words like "inhibited" and "introvert" came into his mind as he pushed through the crowd in the lobby, and he shook his head. He knew a lot about nerves from that first disastrous experience in the army.

Chaos reigned when he opened the stage door again, and with man's ability to push his own affairs aside, the quality he had told Penny most women lacked, he straightened everything out. Then he crossed the set and went down a long corridor to Penny's dressing room.

She was ready for the next act, all in white this time, and calm and sure. "Is it going all right?" she asked. "Do people like it? Did Carrol and David like it?"

"Yeah, everyone thinks it's swell," he answered.

"David, too?"

"Umhum." There were still two acts to go. Her mind must be clear for those two acts. All her emotion must be given to them, all her thoughts, and he said truthfully, "He'll tell you so later, after he's seen it all." Then he pulled the V in her robe a little nearer the center of her small curved breast and added lightly, "Lord, but I'm glad you're so bubbly and know how to let your worries out. I'm even glad you're a little nutty."

CHAPTER VIII

PENNY sat quite still beside Josh as they drove toward Gladstone. The rousing success of the play was but a blur in her memory. Last night it had been important. The mad scene of revelry backstage had been important, with actors hugging each other and old Mr. Cottingham doing a jig, his old bones nimble, his heart happy from congratulations that were more stimulating than an injection of adrenalin. Flowers, telegrams, white gloves applauding, people blocking her dressing room door—it had all been wonderful. Then Josh had said, "Pen, I'd rather you didn't stay for the party," and the fun had ended.

"Why not?" she had asked. "Carrol and David will be here in a minute and they're going to stay in town. They've planned to spend the night at the Waldorf and we can all sleep late."

"They didn't come in, darling," he had answered carefully. "Carrol has a cold or something, and I thought we'd drive out in the morning."

Carrol had more than a cold; Penny knew it, even though Josh's tale had unfolded slowly in a succession of minor shocks. It was as if he set off his dynamite a stick at a time, cleaning up the debris after each little blast, making everything neat and sightly, before he moved on and wrecked a whole mountain.

Carrol. Quiet controlled Carrol. Penny looked out at the flowing countryside and said in a small voice, "She never goes to pieces. She didn't cry much when her father died and she didn't cry at all when David went off to war. I did. I cried till I was a blob. And when we sat in the hospital waiting to hear about Davy, she was the calmest one of all. She went right on knitting his sweater. She was stronger *then* than David."

"Yes, I know she was, but it hurt her."

"And I'm always telling her my troubles. I feel terrible because I've poured them on her."

"That wouldn't do it, darling. You haven't done anything to hurt her." Josh put on speed to pass a car before a curve, and said, "She's steeled herself for a long time and it's the letting go that got her. It's the untying of a lot of knots she kept hidden."

"Was that why you said you're glad I emote?"

"Umhum."

She nuzzled her cheek into his shoulder, then sat up straight again. "You and Carrol are alike sometimes," she said. "You didn't talk much before I got you; you were pretty knotty, too, you know; but you're better, now. If I'd been *you* when I didn't want to be in the play, I'd have told me a lot of things about myself. I'd have made me do it, which was the way it was going to be in the end."

"And would I—you—would you," he asked, confused, "have been happy, had I done it?"

"No. I'd have been mad, clear through, and hurt. I'd have thought you didn't love me."

"So there we are." He turned the car through the gates of Gladstone, and said, as they wound along the wooded driveway, "Everyone has his own way of working things out.

Carrol has hers. It may not be yours or mine or Davids, darling, but it's a brave way. She hung on and saw the thing through. I think she's entitled to a rest and coddling, but it's a shame she has to suffer."

He stopped the car and Perkins came out on the terrace with a grave face. "Good morning, Miss Penny," he said, holding open the car door. "Mr. MacDonald. I'm glad you've arrived. Miss Carrol knows you're coming."

"How is she, Perkins?" Penny slid out and stood on the wide stone step, waiting anxiously for his answer. It could mean very little, but when he said, "She's doing well, I'm told," she ran across the terrace and into the wide carpeted hall. "David?" she called softly, looking into the drawing room where the portrait of Carrol's beautiful mother smiled down from above the mantle, then up the stairway at the two landings and stretch of bannister along the upper hall. "David?"

There was no answer, so she dropped her light tweed coat on a chair and ran up the steps. A starched nurse was just opening the door to Carrol's room; and as she stood looking at her, Penny remembered the night she had stood on the very same spot, staring at the very same scene. It was little Davy's door that had opened then. It had opened for two interns with a stretcher that had a small mound under its white blankets.

"Please," Penny said in a whisper, and the nurse turned and closed the door again. "I'm her sister-in-law," she explained, tiptoeing closer, glad the nurse had a bright, round face and looked capable and kind.

"Mrs. MacDonald, oh, yes. I'm Miss Salter, and Mrs.

Parrish is expecting you. She has been anxious about your coming because she thought you shouldn't try to, but she's very happy, too. Just—don't tire her."

"I won't." Penny took a deep breath and opened the door.

The room was bright with sunshine. A lace coverlet was folded over the end of a blue satin chaise lounge, silver toilet articles caught sunbeams on the white dressing table, and at first glance Carrol looked as she always had, sitting up in the big bed, her hands outstretched. But her cheeks were white, her eyes brighter than they should be, and she called urgently, "Come here. Quickly."

"I'm here, darling." Penny ran to the side of the bed and gripped the hands that clung to hers. "Hold on."

"It's happening again," Carrol said through clenched teeth. "Miss Salter went away. Talk. *Talk!*"

So Penny began about the play. She told everything that had happened. She even told about the flowers, the silly way Fritz bowed and Mr. Cottingham danced. She let her voice rise and fall, and she watched the pain slowly drain from Carrol's face. It became calm again, and Carrol released one hand and reached for a piece of cotton soaked in spirits of ammonia.

"I sniff it," she said. "It helps." Then she lay back on her pillows and apologized, "I'm awfully sorry, Pen, but I get so frightened when I'm left alone. It's silly. I keep telling myself it's silly, but I can't stop the fear when it starts. David calls it my 'quavers.'"

"Where is he? David, I mean."

"He had to take Davy to the hospital." She smiled and looked so happy that Penny wondered if she had dreamed the five minutes that had gone before. "You know that

Davy's all right, don't you?" she asked. "He's taken quite a few steps alone and has the cutest pair of little crutches to use when he's tired. He won't need even those very long. She took a deep breath through her piece of cotton, and ended, "It was seeing his precious little legs moving along without the braces that did it. I'd waited so long to see them do it that something snapped and I passed out. Silly, wasn't it?"

A tear rolled down her cheek and caught in the dimple of her smile, and Penny leaned over to wipe it away. "It wasn't silly at all," she answered. "I fall apart if one of mine gets a bump. That's what I've tried to tell you all these years— mothers live in their children." Conversation was still needed, for Carrol held her one hand tightly, so she said, "But you're going to have to learn to let go. Dump your troubles on David or me. I'm about as strong as a feather bed, but David's a big, sturdy guy; he'll hold you up."

Her remark brought a laugh, thin and short, but a laugh, and she felt more rewarded than when one of her speeches rocked a whole theater with mirth. Carrol's clasp loosened, and she answered, almost dreamily, "Dear, wonderful David. I'm terribly ashamed to say it, Pen, but the silly pill's beginning to work. I'm sort of sleepy and fuzzy."

"All right, darling, I'll go and let you rest."

"No, don't." Her hand was clutched again, then freed. "Just stand in the door and call Miss Salter," Carrol begged, her eyes too wide awake again. "Don't leave till she comes."

"I won't." Penny stood up and moved slowly. She strolled across the room, talking softly over her shoulder, and beckoned to the nurse who was sitting in the wide square hall. Then she went back and dropped a light kiss on Carrol's white cheek. "Would you like us to cable Mums to come home

and be with you?" she asked. "She's such a wonderful help
to me when I'm under the weather, and she'd love an excuse
to fly home."

"Of course not, Pen!" The words sounded more like Carrol than anything she had said, so far, and she went on in a
practical voice, "I'm only tired. There hasn't been a night
when I haven't slept with one ear listening for Davy, and if
I can lie here for a week and get rested, I'll be all right. I'll
be a better mother to little Lang."

Penny stood by the bed and nodded. "There's some of
your trouble," she said sagely. "You've worn yourself out
and you have some foolish idea that you've neglected your
baby; that you've given all of yourself to Davy. But you
haven't. Lang isn't old enough to care or remember. That's
what Josh tells me. As long as his meals are on time and he
has all the comforts of life, a baby doesn't care about anything else."

"You don't think he feels that I—love Davy too much?"
Sleep was gone and Carrol sat up to ask a question she had
to hear answered. "Pen?" she whispered, "do you ever feel
you give more to one child than the other?"

"My heavens, yes!"

Penny answered and smiled. "If one's sick it gets all my
attention. The other one has to shift for itself; but they take
turn about. Let's only hope that Lang will be a disgustingly
healthy child and won't have his turn." She knew the blue
eyes looking up into hers held another unspoken question
and she tried to answer it by saying, as best she could, "Perhaps you think Davy means more to you than Lang does,
but that isn't true, Carrol. He was born while David was overseas, and was sunny and sweet, and such a comfort. You've

had him longer and know him better, and he looks like David, that's all. Langdon Houghton is going to grow up to be your father over again. Then you'll have your father and David in them, and each will have his own place in your heart. Believe me, darling, I know. I have two, and they're as different as day and night. Along with letting your system wear down," she scolded, "you have a bad case of conscience." Penny patted herself on the chest and said, "That's Dr. Mac-Donald diagnosing."

"Thanks, Pen." Carrol sighed and closed her eyes again. "It has troubled me so," she whispered tiredly. "I've thought I loved Davy more. I didn't care what happened as long as he got well. I never got up with Lang at night, or fixed his bottle or did any of the things I always did for Davy. I just made sure he was taken care of and . . . and. . . ."

"You'll enjoy him now. When you get your frazzled nerves unfrazzled, you can fuss over him. I think that will do you more good than anything, so hurry up and rest. I'd better let you start," she said, conscious of the nurse standing by the window, waiting.

"You've helped me so much, Pen."

"I'm glad. It's a new role, I assure you." Penny leaned over and smoothed back the pale blonde curls. If I ever help anyone," she whispered, "the patient should be cured." Then she tiptoed out and down the stairs.

Josh was waiting in the library at the back of the hall, and had been reading. "What did you find out?" he looked up to ask.

"Well, she. . . ." Penny frowned and sat down on a long leather couch opposite him. "I wish David would come home," she said. "I'd like to tell him to keep Lang in the room a lot, plump him down on the bed you know, and let him toddle around and get into things. They ought to *both* be in there, Davy and Lang, and *squabble.*"

"That sounds just the treatment for a nervous breakdown." He put his magazine on a table but she only went on frowning in a perplexed silence.

"Perhaps, I'd better leave David a note," she decided at last, "if we can't wait. Carrol needs to rest a lot, but she needs some gayety, too. Nothing's been very gay around here. Sickness," she added, "is about the most ungay thing I've ever run into. It's depressing."

"But happens in the best of families."

"And there's no sense in carrying it on when it's over." She was talking to herself, not to him, and from long experience he sat and waited. "I let you do everything for me," she said thoughtfully, rubbing her fingers up and down her throat. "Of course, I hold a towel for the kids to woops in and poke medicine into them, but afterward, I fall on you. I'm not self-reliant like Carrol is. That's where her trouble lies. David thinks she's wonderful and look what it's done to her. He's a stupid dope and shouldn't treat her as if she knows everything."

She got up and stalked to the desk while Josh relaxed again to watch her. He wondered what she considered self-reliant to mean, as applied to herself, and considered several definitions a dictionary might give to fit her; such as resolute and independent. He even thought of adding a few of his own. Dynamite would be a good one, he decided, also, a person who can cause more confusion than an atomic bomb. He knew David was in for a sisterly sizzling, so took his little black notebook from his breast pocket, and penciled a few words. *"Take it easy, Dave,"* he wrote, *"Think over what Penny says, but don't let it get you."* He tore out the sheet just as she turned around.

"Here's what I said," she announced with a jerk of her head, "I said, 'Carrol's going to be all right, but you don't deserve it. You ought to be like Josh, and think for her, be loving and kind and. . . .' "

"Hey," he interrupted in protest, "is this letter about me or for David?"

"For him, 'so you'd better make the decisions. When she didn't have time for Lang, you should have. You should have made more friends, too, and not been so grumpy.' "

"Oh, now, Pen! Wait a minute."

"Don't you like it?"

"No. Dave Parrish was never grumpy in his life and you know it. He's a thoughtful, swell guy who always tries to do the right thing as much as anyone I know."

"Well, he fussed at me when I didn't want to be in your play. He marched himself over and laid me out." Penny held her letter stiffly before her and he reached across the space between them and took it.

"You can point out the light to him," he said, tearing both her note and his own into shreds, "but not this way." He heard the front door open and close, Davy's piping little voice in the hall, and stood up to throw the pieces of paper into the fireplace. Penny shot by him and out.

"Oh, David," she cried, hurling herself at her brother. "I'm so sorry for you."

David gave her a hasty punch in the rib and reminded her that she had an audience by turning her around to look at the small boy who was being helped out of his coat. "Have you seen our fine son?" he asked, and no one but Josh noticed how worn he looked. "Davy has his own legs back."

"I *know!*" Penny dropped down on the rug as Davy took three important steps to her. "It's wonderful," she said. "Now you can run with Parri. You can play with Lang, too," she added as an afterthought.

"He's a baby." Davy dismissed Langdon in the same way Parri pushed Joshu out of her sandbox, and asked, "Can I go up now and tell Mums what the doctor said?"

"No." Penny answered instead of David. She pulled Davy down on her lap and explained carefully, "Mums is taking a nap. She's just so glad you're well, you know, that she's resting. But when she wakes up, would you take Lang in to see her and show her how cute he is and how well he can play?"

"But he doesn't."

"He will if you teach him. Joshu isn't nearly as old as Lang and he plays lots of games with Parri."

David listened to the conversation with a puzzled expression and Josh walked over to lay a hand on his shoulder and say in a low tone, "Carrol's a bit worried over having neglected Lang, Dave. She talked about it to Penny, so perhaps you should keep him around a lot. I think she wants to fuss over him."

David nodded slowly. "And this one," he added, pointing, "will have to be eased back into his rightful position, which is not that of a baby, but a loved older son. Thanks for telling me."

Josh saw how easily David understood, how clear his thinking was; and when he said, "Time for lunch, Davy. Will you two stay and join us?" Josh pulled Penny up from the floor and answered, "Not today, thanks. I've a pile of work to do before tonight."

"Then I'll have my tray with Carrol."

"Me, too?" Davy looked up but David shook his head.

"Later, son," he answered, with his eyes searching the big rooms as if he were a little lost. "Later," he repeated vaguely.

"Walk out to the kitchen and surprise everyone," Penny suggested, knowing how David felt not to have Carrol here at this glad homecoming, not to share in the careful work she had done. "Go slowly, dear."

"All right." Davy steadied himself by touching chairs and tables as he walked carefully away from them, and when he was safely into the dining room, she said. "Don't worry, darling. Carrol's all right."

"I feel as if it's my fault," he answered. "I slipped up somewhere and didn't give her the support she needed. I failed her."

"You couldn't." Penny suddenly knew she was speaking the truth. "You did everything in the world you could do," she answered. "If anyone's to blame, I think her father is, because of her childhood, when he pushed her out and didn't want her. It makes her afraid of not giving enough to her own children. Remember that, David. There were four of us racketing around and we didn't have time to worry over who got the most love and attention, and Mums and Dad didn't either. We grew up with a give and take, but Carrol was fifteen before her father came to and loved her, and from then on he couldn't do enough for her. He doted on her. That in itself was a shock and makes her know how lonely a child can be. And I think," she said thoughtfully, "that

Carrol will always be a little lonely inside. She's too reserved to let her feelings come out, too grateful for the love she has, too amazed that it happened."

"I see what you mean." David took the coat Josh brought and held it for her. "I'll work on that line," he said. "Family stuff. We're a family and nothing can lick us."

"Right, darling." Penny stood on tiptoe to kiss him, and she said to Josh when they were driving back to town without having seen their own children, "I wish Carrol could have a little girl to fuss over. Boys are nice but they aren't very understanding little creatures. Just think how cute Parri was in Philadelphia, with her starchy skirts sticking out, and curtsying so nicely. Carrol seems like more of the girl type, too."

"You don't always get what you order."

"I know it, but I wish we could."

She sat quietly in her corner on the return drive, and when Josh had left her at home to take a nap while he went on to the theater, she went straight by the window and curled up in a big chair. A very small idea was busy in her mind, so she sat without moving and let it work undisturbed. David had said "family stuff," they had spoken of their own family and the fun they had had as children with their parents rushing in and out. Happy childhood, happy give and take. It all made sense, for that was the way a family should be. The country was healthy for children. It was nice to have a big yard, a brook to wade in, a hill to coast on, bannisters to slide down when you were older. But did that make a family? Was it any good to have those things if your parents couldn't come to see you on a sunny fall morning when they were only two miles away as she and Josh had been today?

THE RELUCTANT HEART

When you had them only in a hit or miss fashion, and on
week ends? Penny shook her head and put her mind back
on the track. A family meant being together, she reasoned,
even if it had to be in the middle of a crowded city. Cities had
parks where children were taken to play, and apartment
houses had elevators that were just as exciting as stairways.
New York was such a city, and it even had a woman who
was making—who would make, she corrected, if pay day
ever came around—a *very* nice salary. A large salary she
didn't need. What, in the name of reason would she use it
for, unless . . . ? Penny hopped out of her chair and dug out
the classified telephone directory. Her idea had grown to a
concrete decision and she wrote down a list of rental agents.
Then she began to dial.

"Naturally," she repeated over and over, "I've heard of
the housing shortage. But there must be an apartment on
Fifth Avenue somewhere. Quite close to a Central Park entrance, with four or five bedrooms and some baths tucked
in. No, not a walk-up, not on a court. Something pleasant
and sunshiny, preferably furnished."

The agents were noncommittal, but she still kept a feeling
of hope. Having decided that the whole MacDonald clan
belonged together, she coaxed and cajoled and refused to
give up. And at last she found a very understanding gentleman who admitted a terrific fondness for her, dramatically
of course; and while her conscience refused to offer a bribe
in the housing racket, she and the agent ended up in happy
accord. In spite of a sellout for months ahead, he had the
promise of two of the four tickets to *One Step to Heaven*
which were hers for each performance, and she had—hope.

"There, you see," she said to her family who stood in a

row on a table and still looked amused. "That's all you have to do. Make up your mind, and it's done."

Penny was not a spendthrift. She had been well trained by the United States Army which is a large and impersonal organization. Uncle Sam sits at the head of it, and while he is an honest old gentleman who dispenses his paychecks each month with meticulous care, he never tucks in a bonus or a Christmas gift, or even a small award for valor. His checks had been prompt on all the army posts where Penny had lived, but they had gone in and out the houses like a breeze. A budget had been almost as important to daily living as the Bible, and it still surprised her to have money in the bank, especially money she had earned.

She sat down again to think about it, to do a little mental arithmetic, to figure just how much she could spend for an apartment and what such a large, expensive move would entail; and by the time Josh's key turned in the lock, she had alerted her staff at home and was mentally settled.

"You didn't rest," he accused, when she jumped up to kiss him. "Have you been sitting here worrying about Carrol?"

"Oh, dear me, no, I forgot her." Penny was conscience-stricken, and she backed away and sat down again. "Wasn't that awful, Josh?" she said, looking up, her eyes wide. "Perhaps I didn't *forget* her, because she was sort of in the back of my mind and caused me to make a decision, but I didn't actually *worry* about her and I should have. I meant to. I meant to plan some nice things to do for her. Do you think I ought to call up?"

"No, I wouldn't." He hung his hat over his own picture

frame and was about to make himself some coffee when her thoughts veered like a derelict ship.

"Thinking about Carrol," she said, made me decide to have a surprise for you. "I mean, I *have* a surprise. I'll know for sure tomorrow or the next day. No, not tomorrow because there's a matinee, and I won't have time to find out, but surely by Thursday. Yes, I'll have it by Thursday."

"Pen. . . ." He stopped halfway to the kitchenette and stood frozen. "You don't mean . . . oh, my gosh."

"But I do. Families have to be families," she tried to explain.

"But not just now." He almost groped his way back to a chair and sank into it. He remembered her remark about wishing Carrol could have a little girl and how cute Parri looked, even her eagerness last year to add Joshu's name to the expense account. If she had decided that the MacDonald family was short a child, it would have one, new play or no; and he could only stare at her. "Oh, Pen," he said.

"But I thought you'd be pleased." They were talking of different subjects and each looked hurt. A quarrel was rare in their lives and Penny had to dig deep into her memory to find even a little one. "I thought you liked your family," she said unhappily.

"I do, dear, I do," he protested, "but not just now." He got up to pace the floor, then forgot what he had risen for and stood looking down at her. "Listen, Pen," he explained, "we have a play on. I didn't ask you to come into the blamed thing but you did. You should have told me this before you started. What am I going to do?"

"Why. . . ."

"This is a business proposition. I've spent a lot of money, I'm in debt. Can't you see that, Pen?"

"I'm sorry." Her lip trembled, and to hide it she turned her face to the window. "I'm sorry," she repeated, more ashamed for him than disappointed. Her beautiful dream had been a bright balloon and Josh had stuck a pin in it like a spoiled, naughty boy, without reason. He didn't want his family with him—it all boiled down to that. The country was the place for children, and this small hole in New York was where one kept a wife. Here, and on a stage. She turned back to study him. "I can't believe it," she said.

She watched him light a cigarette, his hands nervous and snapping at the lighter. He was tired, she knew he was tired, but aching bones were no excuse. Her own feet and back and head and arms had been tired for weeks. It was a glad kind of tiredness. She had been giving Josh something he wanted. She had given him success. "I thought I knew you," she said slowly, "but I guess I don't."

Josh's cigarette had a hole in it and wouldn't burn, and he threw it disgustedly into an ash tray. "Probably not," he answered. "But you always pick a dramatic time to throw a punch. It isn't that I'm not happy about having children, it's just—oh, what's the use!"

He went to the kitchen, banged open doors until he found a cup, then set it down by the sink. "A new baby," he groaned inwardly. How long would Penny stay in the play? Three months? Four? Would it draw without her or would he have to close? How soon would he be out of the red, how much could he cut expenses? He took a jar of soluble coffee from the shelf, stared at its label while he figured, then carried it back into the room with him. "I guess I let you down, Pen," he said carefully. "I'll try to be as happy as you are from now on and we'll weather it."

"I don't want to, now. I'm not interested in it any more."

"Well, you will be. Babies aren't things you welcome one minute then decide to cancel the next." He thought of offering her a reconciliatory kiss, decided it would be out of keeping, and gave her shoulder a pat instead. But it drew gently out from under his hand.

"Mine are," she answered.

"Well, I like 'em, too," he defended. "I like having them around, but it's as I told you, a man thinks of earning a living for them. I've always said that I didn't expect you to help, and that's true. I didn't urge you to come in with me, but it'll sure knock me for a loop to have you quit."

"I won't quit. I'll *never* quit!" Penny clenched her hands and pulled her shoulders back to stare up at him. "Don't think I'm a child," she said. "I'm not the kind who gets mad and takes my doll clothes and goes home. I said I'd be in your play, and I will. I'll stay in it if it lasts as long as Tobacco Road."

"But if the doctor says. . . ."

"I'm not sick and I'm not going to crack up like Carrol." She took the jar from his unprotesting grasp and marched out to the pantry with it. "I'm pretty sturdy," she called back, finding a spoon and measuring lavishly. "I may not be very pleasant for the next few years but I won't cry on your shoulder, you may be sure of that. Do you want cream in this?"

"I don't care." Josh watched her slap a pan of water on the electric grill, tap her foot impatiently while it warmed.

She found the cream, began to pour the tepid liquid, and said with her back to him, "I'll do everything I can to please you, but there's one thing I'll have to insist on. You'll have to drive me out home every night if it kills you. Since you won't let me have the children in *here* with me, I'll go out to them. Here," she walked back and poked the drink at him.

"Thanks," he answered, taking it and wondering if he could get it down. It looked so strange and had brown clots of undissolved coffee floating on top. "I don't care if you have them here. I'd like them, too, if we had a place to put them; but New York's so full. You might try," he went on, to postpone the moment of drinking. "Well, here's to your health."

The cup moved slowly toward his mouth but she pulled it down. "Josh!" she cried, "Have you gone crazy?"

"Not that I've heard of *yet,* but I might have if you hadn't saved me from this mess. What did you put in it, poison?" he asked, deciding to make light of the whole situation, to put them back on a happy plane again. "Have you relented and are letting me live?"

Penny was not amused. "Why did you suddenly change your mind?" she wanted to know. "Why did you say you'd like to have the children here—after you made it so plain you didn't want them?"

"I didn't say I didn't want them. I'd be glad to have them here, but you didn't ask me."

"Yes, I did. You said. . . ."

"Now, listen, Pen." He laid his free hand gently on her arm and pleaded earnestly, "Let's not fight again. Let's sit down and I'll drink this confounded drink. I'm happy, believe me, I'm happy." He tried to guide her but she refused to move, so he added as a boost, "I want the children here and I'm even pleased about the new baby."

"What new baby?"

THE RELUCTANT HEART

"Why the one you said—the one you—" It occurred to Josh that he might have misinterpreted her statement, and he said helplessly, "I don't know."

"Do you *want* a new baby?"

"Lord, no. I thought you did."

"Why?"

She stood and looked at him, puzzled and trying to figure out what was in his mind, until he shrugged. "Darned if I know," he said. "Something you said about having a surprise and—well, the children, and. . . ." He stopped and grinned. "We *aren't* having a baby?"

"Oh, you're so silly." Penny took the coffee and tasted it. "It's awful," she gulped, returning it hastily. "If you'll make a new one, we'll start all over." She followed him back to the sink and leaned against it. "I have a surprise for you," she announced importantly, watching the contents of the cup go down the drain. "I'd planned to tell you on Thursday. Now, you're supposed to answer."

"Is it nice?" he asked, obediently.

"Wonderful." And at that she moved right in. She pushed between his busy hands and laid her head against his chest. "Let's never fight again," she whispered. "Let's never be disappointed in each other. I was disappointed in you, and you were in me. For just a few minutes," she said, looking up, "we were each filled with bitterness. And in those few minutes our love snapped. That's a wicked thing to do to love. It's letting static in on the beam. The steady stream of our love was broken."

"Not broken, darling, because we tuned out the static. The program is complete and clear again."

"Then let's keep it that way."

"Right!"

He washed out his cup and measured coffee while she leaned against him; and she said while he worked, "If the man I talked to on the telephone can find us an apartment, will you go with me to look at it—*Thursday,* I hope?"

"I'll even treat you to a taxi. Where are we planning to live?"

"On Fifth Avenue, close to the Park." Penny let him add water that was boiling nicely now and tagged along when he carried his steaming cup to their favorite chair by the window. "Before you get too enthusiastic," she said, when he was safely seated and there was a little room left for her to crowd in beside him, "I'd better explain that it's going to cost quite a lot."

"It's cheaper than having a baby. *Anything's* cheaper than that."

He took a satisfied sip and she stretched out her legs to brace herself on the inadequate spot she sat on. "Well, maybe so," she admitted reluctantly, "but you don't get as much for your money."

"Such as?"

"Rent. That much we have to figure on, and upkeep out in the country. Then we'll have to buy a new station wagon," she enumerated, "to go back and forth on weekends; and perhaps have an extra man or a cook."

"What happened to Minna? She looked healthy enough the last time I saw her and a new wagon ought to be strong enough to cart her around."

"Well, if she marries John, she won't want to come in. Or if she doesn't, I thought I'd bring him in where she could keep on courting him."

"But he doesn't want to get married."

"How do you know?"

"I asked him." Josh enjoyed the surprised stare she risked her balance to turn on him, and asked with equal pleasure, "Do you know who the girl is whom he dates at night?"

"No, who?"

"His granddaughter." He took another sip from his cup and kept her waiting while he savored it to the full. "He baby sits," he ended.

"Are you *sure?*"

"Yep. The granddaughter's husband's in a Veteran's hospital and John stays with the children while she goes to see him."

"Where's his wife? And why didn't he ever tell us so I could help them?"

"Help whom?" he asked. "John, the granddaughter or the veteran?"

"All of them, silly. Oh, I remember now, he did tell me he'd had a wife who died years ago. Does he still carry the torch?"

"I guess so. He says he's a grandpappy and happy about it. He likes helping support them. So I think you're out of luck, Mrs. MacDonald."

"I think so, too." Penny laughed and added, "But not as much as Minna. I wish I'd ploughed in and asked John like you did." She slewed around again to regard him. "You're quite all right," she praised, "though I could have done it if you hadn't kept me so busy rehearsing. You putter around and get things done while I work," she scolded.

His coffee was gone and he set the empty cup on the window sill, then lifted Penny's brown hair and kissed the back of her neck. "Sweet child," he said gently, "it's time to work now. It's time for us to eat and go to work. I'm sorry, but it is."

"I'm not."

The street outside was covered by its gray blanket of evening dusk. Lights twinkled from other buildings; and she leaned forward, her arms resting contentedly on her knees. All this would end soon; this scurrying out to dinner and on to work. By careful management she could put her children to bed as would any other mother. Some mothers would go to the movies, some play bridge, some would vary it by an evening out at the theater and watching Penny Parrish. Leaving her children when they were asleep, Penny told herself, wasn't so very different from kissing them good night and going downstairs to read a magazine. And there would be her days, long days, with Sunday and all of Monday in the country. "On Wednesday and Saturday," she said aloud, "I'll go to my bridge club. Lots of mothers go to their bridge clubs." Then she hugged her knees and explained, "I was thinking. I was pretending again."

"Like it?"

"I love it. I wish Carrol could have as much as I have. I'd rather have my life the way it is, and work two afternoons a week, than go to a million bridge clubs. Oh, I hope we can move this week!"

CHAPTER IX

THE Wednesday matinee was well under way when Josh opened Penny's dressing room door and poked his head in. She was resting before her call for the second act, and he said quickly, "If you don't mind, honey, I think I'll run out to Gladstone. Nothing to worry about," he added hastily, as she sat up on the chaise longue. "Not a thing, I mean it. I have some business with Dave, that's all. Show business," he explained, when she still looked unsure, and at that she leaned back again and let him go on. "I've ordered dinner sent in for you so you won't have to eat in a restaurant alone, and I thought I might drive you out home tomorrow and let you have a day with the kids. Okay?"

"Okay." She smiled and nodded. "And give Carrol my love. Tell her I'll be over to see her tomorrow, right after lunch. You're sure she's all right?"

"I'm sure."

"Then run on." The call boy was making his rounds and she blew Josh a kiss. "Don't drive too fast," she cautioned, and watched the closing door shut out his grin.

The day had begun like any other and was plodding along like a reliable dray horse making his rounds. Josh's sudden departure had only quickened its pace, but the message Ma gave her when she climbed out of her wheel chair at the end of the second act turned it into a race. "There was a man here from the agency," Ma said, before Penny was even inside the dressing room. "He has an apartment for you to see, and he

[163]

said the people who own it have already taken off for Holly-
wood. The superintendent's waiting to show it to you and
you have to make up your mind in a hurry. Tonight, I guess,
because someone else wants it. I put the address on your
shelf."

"Where is it?"

"Right there."

"I don't mean the card. Where's the apartment? Oh, yes,
it says Fifth Avenue. Three bedrooms, two baths. And Josh
has just gone! It isn't a very big apartment, is it?"

"It's still an apartment." Ma was bringing out the red
wool dress and Penny laid the card down reluctantly. "I
wish I could go this minute," she said. "Drat working!"

She repaired her make-up with quick, expert fingers and
said, with one eye squinted for a new dash of mascara,
"You'd better go out and telephone during the act. Call the
agent and tell him I'm coming just as soon as I finish here.
And tell Brooks to have a taxi for me and to postpone my
dinner. Heaven knows *when* I'll get back."

She was so excited all through the third act of the play
that she ran up the steep wooden steps to the balcony which
was, as far as the audience could see, a stair landing; and she
was panting and ahead of time. Her husband was making
important love to the big-eyed *ingénue,* and Penny, as his
disinterested wife, stood behind the canvas and meditated on
other things. "I could put the two children in one room," she
mused, "and Trudy in the other. But what would I do with
Minna?" Her mind heard the conversation going on below
her and she even made sure her belt dipped properly in the
back while she figured on her *ménage* and looked at stealthily
moving figures across from her in the wings. A Leko spot

was acting up and an electrician crawled toward it under a window.

"I maintain a large home," she heard her husband say, "because I'm a bachelor who likes his comfort." It was almost time and she instinctively moved a step nearer. The spot had decided to function, the electrician crawled back and she looked beyond him at a tall young officer who grinned at her. They stared at each other for several seconds before she recognized him. "My heavens, it's Terry Hayes!" she gasped. "Terry *Hayes.*" Then her husband said, "I need a wife," and she walked to the center of the landing.

"You have one." Her voice was controlled, each step careful as she held the rail, but her mind was whirling. Where had this suitor from her past come from? Penny was too good an actress to wonder long, and by the time she had reached the bottom step she was working the play to its crescendoed climax and had forgotten the man she had seen.

But when the curtain had dropped, when she was finished bowing to the right, to the left, with long, sweeping smiles for the balcony, she remembered him, and plunged off the stage. "Terry, you dear!" she cried, catching both his hands. "It's like old times to have you turn up. *Where* have you been?"

"It's good to see you, lamb-child." It was his usual greeting after one of his prolonged absences and he held her off and studied her. "Success fits you like a glove," he decided. "You're more vivid than ever. How's Josh?"

"Wonderful. He had to go out to David's but he'll be back." There was so much she wanted to tell him, wanted to hear, that she linked her arm through his and drew him toward her dressing room. But in the corridor, she stopped. "I can't sit and talk," she suddenly remembered, "I have to go see an apartment."

"Want me to tag along?"

"Oh, *would* you?" It was fun to be with him; it was like being a girl again, at West Point, at Fort Knox, Fort Arden, at all the army posts where Terry had made her feel young and exciting; and she cried, "I won't be a minute! Look, why don't you sit in one of our fine chairs on the set—or better still, go out and round us up a cab? I'll hurry."

She danced along her corridor, and said to Ma, "Terry Hayes is back!"

"That handsome thing?" Ma shook her head and looked pained. "He always brings trouble," she grumbled, taking the red dress Penny peeled off. "I wish I'd seen him before you did so I could have sent him packing."

"He'd have kidded you and made you feel like a million." Penny sat down before her shelf and said through a smear of cold cream, "You're jealous because he came to see me. I think you've always been secretly jealous."

"Hmph!" Ma gave a snort that stirred a red lace ruffle on the dress and waddled over to her pressing board. "Here today and gone tomorrow," she muttered. "Begging you to love him, begging me to help him. You're safely married now, and if he stirs up Josh. . . ."

"He won't." Penny laughed and turned around to say, "Terry got over me five years ago. He knew we'd have ended up in a fight. We never did anything but fight, anyway. He's darling, though, Ma."

"Yeah, about as darling as a bolt of lightning. Just see that he doesn't strike you."

"I will."

THE RELUCTANT HEART

Penny was dressed in five minutes flat. She had her card in her purse and Terry had a cab.

"Where do you want to go?" he asked, and watched with amused patience while she dug out the address. "Still the same old fumble-duddy," he teased, when she crammed the mess back into her bag. "How does Josh stand it?"

"He thrives on it," she retorted. "Now tell me all about yourself. I have two children for you to see, two beautiful children; Mums and Dad are in Germany; Davy had polio; and Carrol's been sick. We're planning to move just as soon as I see this apartment and. . . ." She stopped her rushing flow of words and laughed. "How are you?" she asked.

"Fine, fine." He looked it. His skin was bronzed, his eyes blue and clear, and his service cap shaded his face at a correct cavalryman's slant. "I just got in from England," he volunteered. "I've been over there most of the time since the war but I'm home to stay. I'll be stationed in Washington."

"Are you married?"

"No. I was, though, for a while."

The cab chose an unfortunate moment to stop for she wanted to hear more. His last remark had unraveled his matted affection for her because, having been married, he could no longer insist that she was never out of his thoughts; and while they waited for a doorman to call the superintendent of the building, she said frankly, "We want to see a lot of you from now on. I have to settle this apartment business quickly, so let's keep our minds on it, and after we're through . . . will you take me to dinner?"

"Just what I'd planned."

Terry Hayes loved Penny because she was so completely herself. All her thoughts poured out, her feelings; and she had often reminded him of an artist's palette that was daubed and splattered with bright colors. Each mood was a bright splotch until it was mixed with another, blended into a startling combination or toned into a shade. Just now, he decided, she was orange. She was an orange flame as she darted from room to room; and he wondered what mixture would be needed to reduce her to a domesticated tan.

"I think I like it," she decided, when the superintendent had gone off to answer another message and she stood by one of the windows in the living room, looking out at the lake in Central Park. "Of course, two of the bedrooms are frightfully small and ours is enormous, but we could manage. The grand piano looks nice even though I can't play it, and I'd have to take out most of the beautiful vases and imported figurines. It would break us up to replace them. And I'm not just sure how the kids will react to pale rose carpeting."

She turned to study the room while he studied her. He moved one of the heavy green silk drapes aside and sat down on the wide window sill to do it. She had pushed back her funny little hat that was nothing but deep velvet flowers held flat by tulle, and her curls were soft around her serious face. She was vivid in the setting western sun; and sitting there, watching the thoughtful way she considered the room, an old ache returned. He had thought he was cured.

"Penny?" he asked, and she turned around. "Are you happy?"

"Completely." There was no hint of doubt in her answer. Her eyes lost their look of contemplation and lighted up. "Are you?" she made the mistake of asking.

"I don't know. Do you remember when you asked me in the cab if I'd been married? Would you like to hear about it?"

"Why, yes. I don't think the supe's ever coming back so we've plenty of time. I'd like to hear, Terry," she said, and sat down beside him.

"I met a girl in England," he began. "It was just after the war when I went over to be assistant military attaché, and I met her at a reception. She. . . ." He paused, stared thoughtfully down at his brown shoes, then went on, "She reminded me of you. She had gray eyes and light hair, but she looked like you. It may have been the way she held her head and the fearless, interested way her eyes looked at everyone, but I knew I had to meet her. I found a friend of mine to introduce us and we left the party and sat in a restaurant, and talked. She even talked like you, and thought like you—and I got it into my head that she was you. We were married a month later; and Pen,—she wasn't you."

"Oh, Terry, I'm so sorry you weren't happy."

"She quit being a lot of fun and went social. We couldn't browse around or walk in the rain because we had people coming to tea. She wanted a car instead of hiring the funny old taxi cabs that are a tradition in London and she was always having her hair set. Of all strange things to quarrel about, and we quarreled about plenty, that was the one that finished us. She came home looking like a store dummy and I told her so. I even told her she was only a bum imitation of a wax figure and of the girl I really loved—you."

Penny was quiet as she faced the room which was in complete shadow now. What little light came in was blocked by their two figures, and she said sadly, "That wasn't fair. I don't know the girl, Terry, but I'm sorry for her. You do like to fight."

"Only with you. I like to battle with you because you're so

funny. You have a swell sense of humor and we always sent each other an orchid when we won. I did it once to Pamela, and she didn't get the point at all. She thought I was sorry."

"I don't blame her. How did she know it was meant to be a joke? Oh, Terry," she urged wistfully, "couldn't you try again?"

"No, not a chance. She wouldn't leave merry old England and she knows I was a heel and only imagined she was someone else. She's too smart to be fooled. Oh, lamb-child," Terry took her hand from her lap and laid his cheek in its palm, "I wish I hadn't come back."

"I—wish so, too."

"I'm still jealous of Josh. I'm jealous of this apartment and of everything you do. I can't get over it, Pen. I've tried. I married a girl, and I've tried."

The apartment was spoiled. It wasn't Josh's apartment now, it was Terry's. He had stolen it; and she said unhappily, "I know love hurts. It hurt me terribly when I thought Josh wasn't going to love me, but—I don't believe I mean that much to you. Truly, I can't. You did love Pamela. You did, no matter what you say," she repeated, when he tried to protest. "You saw me today with a lot of glamour, with grease paint and people clapping. Perhaps that's the way you always see me. But sometimes I'm tired and cross and have my hair up on bobby pins. You wouldn't like that me. You wouldn't like the one who balked at being in the play, who worries and doesn't want to leave her children. There are lots of me's that you wouldn't like, Terry."

"I love you." He reached out and gathered her into his arms; and she accepted it passively, neither pulling away from him or relaxing against him.

THE RELUCTANT HEART

This was the same Terry who always had got what he wanted, and she felt a gentle pity for Pamela who didn't understand him. "Please don't," she said, when his hand touched her cheek. "I'll kiss you if you want me to, but I'd rather not. It would be like a stage kiss, with my mind on other things."

At that, he pushed her away and stood up. "You're cruel, lamb-child," he said gruffly, and she answered:

"I don't think so. I don't know just what you expected me to do—throw myself into your arms and tell you I've been pining away for five years, or to be cheap and sly. If you want me truthful, I'm truthful. I'm sorry for you, terribly sorry, but I don't think you quite believe all this yourself. You're simply putting on an act."

His hands grasped her wrists and pulled her up. His grip was strong and she whimpered, "Oh, Terry, you're hurting me." Then his lips crushed against hers.

A light clicked on in the foyer. "Lady?" a voice called. "Have you finished looking, yet?"

"Yes." Penny pulled away and walked the length of the long room. "It's very nice," she said shakily, to the fat old man who was in a hurry to be rid of her. Her voice quivered, and she tried to control it as she added, "My husband and I will talk it over and let the agent know first thing in the morning. Will that be satisfactory?"

"I guess so, though it'd be better if you could decide before I show it again." He looked at Terry as if waiting for him to come forward and make up his mind, and Penny felt herself blushing.

"We—we'll let you know tomorrow," she said, and hurried into the elevator; but he still persisted.

"Do you like it, mister?"

"Very much." Terry followed them into the cage and leaned against its wall. "Very much," he repeated, and looked humbly at Penny.

She told him good-by on the sidewalk, with the superintendent and the elevator boy watching through the glass and the doorman whistling for a cab. "We can't have dinner together, now," she said. "You aren't a Terry I can know. I'm sorry, because I wanted us all to be together and have fun."

"If you'll forgive me, Pen. . . ."

"I can't." She turned away to hide hurt tears but he followed her to the taxi.

"Please try," he coaxed. "I'll be at the Biltmore for a few days. Please, won't you call me there?"

"No." She leaned back in the cab and he closed the door. "Drive to the *Alvin* theater," she directed, and left him standing there, looking shamefaced and forlorn.

Ma knew something had gone wrong when Penny came in and quietly closed the door. "Where's the great Hayes?" she asked, whisking a napkin from a tray that stood on a table and lifting silver covers from the dishes.

"He had another engagement." Penny went to a wash basin in the corner, ran the water and scrubbed Terry's kiss from her lips. "I have a headache, Ma," she said. "I'd like to rest a bit, if you don't mind going out. Wednesday's such an awfully long day."

"That it is. Did you and Hayes fall out?"

"Please, Ma."

"Okay."

Ma Harkins pulled a chair to the little table and gently closed the door. And when she was safely alone, Penny crossed the room and turned out the lights. She groped her way back to the chaise longue and hid her face in its pillows. Her dinner congealed in its dishes, the coffee cooled, and she was still huddled there when Josh came in at eight o'clock.

"What's wrong, darling?" he asked, turning on the bright lights that showed her flushed cheeks and streaks of tears.

"Oh, Josh!" Penny sat up and held out her arms. "Hold me tight," she wept. "I've had the most horrible afternoon."

The story came out in pieces while he sat beside her. She began at the end and put the introduction in the middle; and when she had reached some sort of conclusion, he asked, "Are you crying over Terry, or what?"

"Why, I think it's *awful!*" she said, and sat up. "Of *course* I'm not crying over him. He's ruined everything. The idea of his kissing me in an empty apartment, right behind your back! I can't rent the apartment, now, because I'd always be seeing him in it and remembering the way he kissed me. I'm not sorry for *him,* I'm just ashamed and disgusted. I'm sorry for *us* because we can't *move!*"

Her words, with all her staccatoes, made him laugh. "Listen, babe-in-arms," he said, "it wasn't sporting, I'll grant you that. But I can't blame the guy for wanting to kiss you— I find it very pleasant, myself. I think he's honestly in love with you. Does that ease your conscience?"

"No. He didn't have to kiss me," she argued. "He could have told me he loved me and let it go at that."

"Would that have been any more honorable?"

Penny thought a moment and shook her head. "I guess it wouldn't," she admitted.

"Things like this happen, darling, and we can't wrap ourselves in cellophane to keep life from touching us. The little events don't matter and can't hurt us as long as we know our love is too strong to be hurt."

"But aren't you furious at him? Don't you hate him for kissing me? I have his kiss right here on my mouth. He *kissed* me!"

Josh's eyes searched hers, then he bent over and pressed his lips to hers. "There," he said, lifting his head. "Does that take it away?"

She smiled and considered. "Some," she conceded. "If you'd try it again." But he only rumpled her hair.

"Tell me," he asked, "did you really like the apartment?"

"Yes—no. Terry ruined it." She was still stubbornly possessed by one idea, and sat straight up with her hands clasped around her knees. "I should think you'd hate him," she fumed.

"I don't see why. Did you hate the obvious Neda?"

His eyes were laughing at her until she could do nothing but sputter. "You knew she was after me," he went on, enjoying her confusion. "Not because of my fatal charm but because I was a good catch in the theatrical world. She'd have taken me away from you if she could have and made me husband number three. Did you mind?"

"No."

"Did you hate her?"

"No," Penny admitted again, reluctantly. "I was rather sorry for her. I had you and she didn't, and I thought she was pitiful." She made her statements seriously, then, struck by a sudden thought, glared at him and demanded, "Did she ever *kiss* you?"

"Nope, but she hounded me with loving glances and you

might even say she cuddled whenever she had a chance. She wasn't quite as impetuous as Terry but the situation was the same. She tried."

"But she didn't get you. That's the point," Penny said, nodding her head up and down. "I *knew* she couldn't get you. I was very sure and smug."

"So am I. That's why anyone who tries to come between us isn't worth worrying about. He'll lose."

"Lose." Penny repeated the word thoughtfully, savoring it to its full. "Lose." Her eyes widened and she cried, "Why, I won, didn't I? Terry's the one to be embarrassed and ashamed, to hate himself. I haven't anything on my conscience at all."

"Not a thing. Shall we ask him to dinner instead of making an issue of it? Just to save you both any future embarrassment? You'll be bound to meet sometime, you know."

"I won." Penny clasped her knees again and considered the invitation. "By golly," she said, "I'll send him an orchid. That will show him what I think of his silly actions, and will make him know that you know all about it."

"What does my knowing have to do with it?"

"I want him to know I've told you. We'll invite him to dinner and he'll see that we aren't mad. I'd invite him right up to that apartment if I could—if I could get moved in time."

"Which you can't." Josh took one of his personal calling cards from his wallet and gave her his fountain pen. "Here, write your card," he said with a grin. "I'll go out and buy your floral tribute. For what night do you want to ask him?"

"Saturday, I think. After the matinee." She tapped the pen against her teeth, frowned in concentration, then scribbled

quickly, *"All is forgiven. Come dine with us on Saturday."*
Her signature was attached with a flourish and she passed
him the pen. "You, too," she said. "So he'll *know.*"

Josh dutifully wrote his name and slipped the card into his
breast pocket. "Nothing more to worry about," he said
lightly. "Nothing to worry about in the first place, except the
poor guy's feelings. Do you think you can eat, now?"

"Yes." She reached out to pat his hand and saw his wrist
watch. "Oh, dear, I've only fifteen minutes until the curtain!
I'll bet Ma's having a fit outside and is afraid to knock. Run,
get her."

Josh went over to open the door and she slid off her sofa.
She ran to her make-up shelf, smeared her face with cold
cream, and forgot to tie a protecting towel around her hair,
or take off her wrinkled dress. "Mrs. Harkins," she said over
her shoulder, stopping Ma's inward rush, "I want you to meet
a very great gentleman. My husband, Mr. MacDonald."

"Pleased to meet him, I'm sure."

The scene was quite different from what Ma had expected
to see, from what she had warned Josh he would find, and she
bustled in on the balls of her feet.

"The pleasure's all mine," Josh answered, and sent her a
wink.

CHAPTER X

THE MacDonalds were moved; all but John and Dog, who stayed in the country. They had lived in the apartment long enough to have it seem like home, to know the staff that ran the building and to have Parri spill a bottle of ink on a bedroom carpet. Minna slept in the room on Thirty-seventh Street and came every morning. She left the little place tidy for Josh who worked there and, because she had quite a distance to travel by subway, Trudy started the children's breakfast.

It was a family rule that Penny must stay in bed until nine. "I think it's silly," she had grumbled at first, getting up and staggering sleepily out to the kitchen where she was more confusing than helpful. "Just riding around in a wheel chair every night can't make me tired."

"Scoot," Josh had returned, pushing her out of his way and reknotting Parri's napkin so she could put her chin over it. "You're entitled to sleep. Do you want to pile up like Carrol?"

"Dear Gussie, no!" And she had fled back to her bedroom, and stayed there.

Carrol was better. Her attacks of panic came less frequently, sometimes more than a week apart, and lighter. She drove into town now and then, and spent long lazy Sundays at Round Tree Farm, leaning back in a chair and watching the children, her hands idle in her lap.

"You don't knit any more," Penny mentioned once, when

they were lounging before a crackling fire and the children were outside, playing in the piles of leaves John had raked. "It seems queer not to see you poking needles in and out."

"I hope I never do again. I used to knit to keep calm and not think. Davy has enough sweaters to last him until he's ten years old, at least, and Lang has, too." She stopped and laughed. "Davy never can wear them all so Lang will have to inherit them."

"How do you like him, now?" Penny asked, daring to touch a subject that was like a boil and needed to be opened. "Lang, I mean?"

"I adore him. You were right, Pen," Carrol answered calmly, "I loved him just as much all the time. I couldn't see it because I was too absorbed in Davy, that's all. They're a nice little team."

They were more than that, for they were part of a good little foursome. Davy ran and played with Parri, and the only one who screamed because he was left behind, was Joshu, who couldn't walk.

Days grew shorter, and Penny's work was easier for her because she had accustomed herself to routine. Up at nine, to bed at twelve. A two o'clock rest while the children napped; and on Wednesdays and Saturdays, dinner in a housecoat on the pale rose rug before a fire.

"Sometimes I feel like an old-fashioned fire horse," she grumbled to Trudy one Saturday morning. "Clang goes the bell and out rush I. Down comes my harness; whip-whip, false alarm; and I'm back again. Nothing like a good blaze ever happens to me."

She was cutting swaths across a table with a dust cloth, and Trudy stopped pushing a carpet sweeper to answer shrewdly, "We often think life's pretty dull; then we look back, years later, to find it wasn't."

"It never was dull in the country. Oh, I'm not complaining," she hurried to say, forestalling anything that might come at her. "I'm satisfied. I did it. But you can't blame me for wishing that something unexpected would happen. I'd even like it if the audience would laugh with a bang some night when I'm doing a tear-jerker speech, or if they'd cry at one of my funniest lines. Variety, my friend," she said, knocking over her father's picture, "is, so I'm told and have learned for myself, the spice of life."

She set the picture upright with a thump just as the doorbell pealed. "Now, who could that be?" she wondered, and felt a little emotional at the unexpected happening.

Trudy snatched her dust cloth and sweeper, and fled; and Penny went into the foyer that had walls papered with birds and always made her feel like chirping, and pulled open the door.

Her younger brother stood there. He wore his gray cadet uniform and held his overcoat over one arm, his round stiff cap against his chest. "Good morning," he said, ignoring her shriek. "You may not remember me, but I'm Robert Parrish. I've been told that I have a sister living in New York and I brought a photograph along so I could identify her."

"Come in, idiot." Penny dragged him inside and pulled his head down by his bright clipped curls. "Bless you, child," she said, "I meant to come see you, truly I did. I was coming next week," she decided, and kissed him.

"I'll bet. If it hadn't been for Trudy I'd have starved to death. I'm darned near starved as it is."

He did look thin. His cheekline had lost its round boyish

curve; and studying him, she thought his blue eyes looked more deeply set than they had. "Poor boy," she said. "Every time I called up, you said you were fine."

"What did you want me to do, burst into tears?" Bobby Parrish was still cross about his treatment. The first year at West Point is always a hard one to weather, and he felt abandoned and abused. He had intended to remain that way for ten minutes, which was two-thirds of the time he had allotted for his call, but Penny's genuine concern over the loose mold of his uniform made him say hastily, "Look, Pen, I'm okay. Don't go into a tizzy."

"But you do look thin. For goodness' sake, sit down and let me ask Minna to make you some pancakes." She tried to take his cap, tried to lead him to the living room, but he only pushed her away.

"Let go of me," he growled. "I don't want any pancakes. I have a date and I'm in a hurry. I only stopped by to say. . . ."

"Would you like to see *One Step to Heaven* this afternoon? You can take your date."

"I'm going to a football game. Gee," he said, shaking his head, "you must be getting old, to forget the Columbia game and the corps coming down. How did you think I got here except with the corps?"

"I hadn't had time even to wonder. We've been occupied with your health, if you remember."

"Oh, yes. Well," he looked around and remarked pleasantly, "some place you have here," then prepared to repeat the message he had come to deliver. "I had a cable from the folks," he said.

At that, Penny got him through the living room archway

and pushed him down on a love seat. "What did they say?" she cried. "Are they all right?"

"They're coming home. Tomorrow."

"Oh, Bobby, stop teasing!" Without giving him a chance to go on, she glared at him. "That's mean," she said, exactly as if he were small again.

"But they are. Here, you can read it." He searched around in the lining of his cap which was the only pocket he had, and produced a piece of crumpled paper. "It's from Mums, and she says Dad's wound has kicked up again—since he fell off a loading platform—and the army's flying them home to Walter Reed. She hopes Tippy can stay here with you."

"Oh, my stars!" Penny disposed of her little sister by mentally parking her on a sofa or sending her home with Minna. "Of course, we'll take her!" she cried, running toward the kitchen and shouting for Trudy, running back for the cable, and ending up in the middle of the room, beaming upon all her photographs. "They're coming home," she breathed. "I can't believe it."

"Well, it's true." Bobby had had a whole evening and the morning to accustom himself to the idea, and he imparted practically, "I telephoned David. He and Carrol will be at the airport. I have to go now."

"But why? You just came. You haven't seen Trudy or the children."

"Listen." To Bobby, Penny was a first grade moron. There had been a time in his life, not so many years before, when she had seemed a fount of wisdom, but that was past. He now lived in a world of disciplined men who controlled themselves; so he said, with careful enunciation, "I have told you. I have a date. I must return to West Point tonight, and I have a date.

I am going to a luncheon at the Waldorf, to a football game, to dinner and dancing—and I have exactly eleven hours and five minutes to do it in."

"I'm sorry, darling." She was contrite. "I know I should bring the children up to see you, and I will. And thank you for taking time out in your busy day to drop by and give me the message. I do appreciate it, Bobby. You could have telephoned, you know."

"Yeah." He made no move to leave and she looked at him doubtfully, wondering why he waited when his haste was so extreme.

"It was thoughtful," she tacked on, thinking he might feel he merited more praise. But he only muttered, "Yep," again, and she suddenly remembered other times when he had shuffled his feet and refused to budge. "Wait till I find my purse," she said through her amusement and his sheepish grin. "I always tip a delivery boy."

"Now *those* are words I like to hear." He followed along behind her and stopped to watch Parri slop red paint on a bluebird, let Trudy fuss over him, and even hoped Joshu was having a pleasant nap. Twenty-five dollars found its way under the snug band in his cap and Penny was restored to her pedestal, her wisdom having proved itself profound.

"Was it worth the trip?" she couldn't resist asking, when he pawed her fondly on the back.

"A rich sister is worth a *lot* of trouble," he answered, standing in the vestibule door and grinning. "An army officer never makes much money so I hope Tippy will chose a career, too. With two of you to support me, I might make out very well and could even afford a wife. Well, thanks."

"Thank *you.*" Penny nodded to him and leaned against the

door while they waited for the elevator. He was such a nice-looking boy and she was so proud of him that she wanted to step out and kiss him. She knew he would hate it, so only stood and watched him step jauntily into the elevator with fine military bearing. "When Joshu grows up," she said to herself, "I shan't be able to hug him either. I can't be always patting him or smoothing his hair. A girl can, his wife can—but I can't. He'd hate it. That's queer. I wonder when Mums found it out and if she had to be careful about remembering it. I can ask her—*tomorrow!*"

The thought was like a sudden pinch that made her jump. "Oh, happy day," she caroled, sailing back across the room; and she said to Trudy, "I haven't felt in such a happy turmoil since we left Round Tree Farm. John can bring the station wagon in and we'll all drive out to Mitchel Field around noon. If Mums and Dad have to go straight on to Washington, we can take Tippy out to the country with us. Oh, Trudy, isn't it *wonderful?*"

"Yes'm, 'tis." Trudy had been almost silent since Bobby had broken his news, and she sat quietly at the kitchen table applying white polish to Joshu's little shoe. "It is," she repeated softly. "My Miz Parrish is comin' back."

"Oh, Trudy, darling." Penny flew across the kitchen and gathered the loving little woman into her arms. "I know this means more to you than to any of us," she said softly. "You've been so patient; and I know you've been lonely and unhappy away from Mums. I don't see what I'd ever have done without you, though."

"It's all right, child. We has to take the army as it comes, its changes and moving around."

"But the waiting is over. If Dad is retired, and I feel sure he will be, we'll all live near one another. I'll hate not having you with me, but. . . ." She suddenly realized what it would mean to her, this losing of Trudy, and gasped, "My goodness! I'll be afraid to stay away from home a minute. I've always felt so safe because I knew you were there."

"We'll be close, child. Your mama and papa will help you, too."

"I suppose so." Had this calamity struck two months ago, Penny knew she would have gone to pieces. She would have canceled the play; she would have stayed in the country like a frightened mother bird on her nest. Now she said in a matter-of-fact voice, "I'd better start looking for a nurse next week so you can train her. Minna can keep her eye on things when I'm not here and can keep me posted."

Minna was stolidly busy at the sink but at the sound of her name she turned around. Parrishes might come and go, MacDonalds might make or lose money in "the play-acting business," but she had a question to ask. It had been uppermost in her mind and she had waited patiently until the proper moment presented itself. Now she said, "I have made plans to be in the village at two o'clock tomorrow, as we always are. Will I be there?"

"Dear me, no," Penny answered, surprised. "How can you be, when we have to meet the family and drive out late?"

"Then I go back with John."

"But why? I'd expected John to wait for us." For a day that had started out to be dull, this one was turning into a terror, and she ran her hand through her hair, and asked, "What do you want to be out *there* for?"

"I go to baby sit."

"That's silly. The children won't be there, we'll have them with us."

"It is not for *our* children," Minna replied importantly. "It is for John's granddaughter. Until we move to town I often baby sit. At first, I sit so John can have some time with his friends in the pool room, but now we play gin rummy. I like it very much."

"Well, I never!" The whole household was falling apart, and Penny looked helplessly at Minna. "Do I hear wedding bells?" she queried.

"Na!" Minna shook her head and let a chuckle ripple over her fat body. "John and me, we are too old," she answered, so coyly that Penny knew she didn't think so. "When Mr. MacDonald asks John to tell me of his granddaughter, I understand many things that have made him seem so forgetful and unpleasant. We are very happy to help a young girl go to see her husband. She is also not a very good cook, so I must be there tomorrow. If John must come to town, especially must I be there."

"Oh, for the love of Pete, *be there!*" Penny followed her words with a laugh, and added, "I'll send John along as soon as I can—at least in time for dessert and the gin rummy," but Minna gravely shook her head.

"Ah, na," she reproved. "On Sunday night the granddaughter comes home and we go to church."

It was all too much. Trudy would be gone, Minna would be skittering out every evening for her baby sitting, and even she and Josh, who were the children's parents, would be off on their own important business. The situation needed consultation, and she dragged out the kitchen step ladder and sat down on it. "Let's work out some things," she began, just as a piercing scream came from the bathroom.

The frightened three raced each other through the hall and found Parri lying on the tiled floor. Her face and dress were covered with spilled powder and the tub was splattered with blood. Penny reached her first and picked her up.

"Look out, child," Trudy warned above the screams. "She's cut her head."

She snatched a towel from a rack, held it against the bleeding gash and kept it there while Penny carried the limp little form into her bedroom. "Hush, darling," Penny soothed, sitting down and trying to part a bloody mat of hair. "You're all right. You just bumped your head, so sit still and let Mummy look."

Parri's terrified screams lessened to sobs, and she wept, "I climbed up on the bathtub. I—I wanted to put on some powder—I didn't mean to fall."

"Of course not, honey—let me see.'

The cut was long but not deep. She could see that much in spite of Parri's hands that kept pushing her fingers away, and she looked up to say in a voice she scarcely recognized as her own, "Hold her for me, Trudy, while I call the pediatrician Carrol always has. He'll probably have to sew it."

The very sound of a doctor started Parri's screams again, but Penny passed her over. She looked calmly through the telephone directory, tried several numbers, and gave up. "I can't reach anyone," she said. "But I saw some doctors' offices in a building down the street. I'll run down there."

Parri was sobbing softly again while Trudy washed the powder out of her eyes and Minna applied damp cloths to the cut. When one was soaked another was laid on, and there seemed to be an endless flow of blood. "Just keep it up till I get back," Penny said, and snatched her beaver coat from the closet.

She ran in and out of three offices before she found a doctor who could leave his patients and go with her; and it seemed hours before she held Parri on her lap again and watched him painstakingly shave away the straight fine hair from the back of the little head. He was a kind young man, and deft, and only asked that she hold the terrified child and keep her hands from reaching up. But at last it was over. Parri wore a white plaster and her tears had stopped.

"There's nothing to worry about," the doctor said practically, repacking his instruments. "No concussion, I'm sure. But you look much the worse for wear, Mrs. MacDonald, and I think you'd better lie down. You're whiter than the little girl is."

"Oh, I'm all right," Penny protested, even though she was afraid she might disgrace herself by fainting; and she wiped clammy perspiration from her forehead. "I never saw so much blood," she said in a voice that sounded very far away and hollow.

"You'd make a good nurse." He held a bottle of smelling salts under her nose and she looked up, blinking.

"Me?" she asked, her nose smarting from the deep sniff she had taken. "I'm never any help in a crisis. The only other time I could have been was when a little girl I was playing with fell out of a tree and broke her arm. I gave one look at the twisted thing and took off. I ran all the way around the block."

Parri leaned against her and she held her close. All during the operation she had kept her eyes on the clock by her bed.

The minute hand had slipped around in a race. Even the hour hand had given a little lurch and a gentle gong had chimed. "Is it all right to give Parri her lunch?" she asked. "It was almost time for her to have it when she fell."

"By all means; but something light. She needs to eat." There was nothing more he could do, and he added, "I'll look in tomorrow, and, if you don't mind my suggesting it, I'd lie down a bit, if I were you. You still look shaken."

"I can't." Penny smiled and shook her head. "I have to go to work and I'm late."

She carried Parri with her as she walked to the door with him, then took her back and turned her over to Trudy. Joshu was playing on the kitchen floor, and she had forgotten all about him. Parri had filled her mind. "Hi, little man," she said, stooping over to kiss him, untroubled by any thought of neglect or of pushing him out of her heart, as Carrol had been. "Look at the cute little patch your sister has on her head."

Parri wasn't sure she liked her patch. It hurt; and she buried her face in Trudy's apron. Trudy rocked her back and forth, patting her and singing, and Penny stood watching them.

"I have to go," she said unhappily. "I feel as if I can't, but I have to."

"Run along. We'll be all right here and I won't let her out of my sight. I wouldn't have this morning," Trudy explained with a sigh, "if it hadn't been for the talk we was havin' an' the excitement, an' all. Go off peacefully, child, but try to eat something first."

"I haven't time." Penny looked down at the blood on her navy blue dress, and added ruefully, "I haven't even time to change. I'll have to go, Trudy. Are you *sure* you and Minna can manage?"

"Ya, we manage." Minna thrust out a sandwich wrapped in waxed paper, said, "put this into your pocket book," and turned back to change Parri's noon dinner to a mid-afternoon egg-on-toast. "I stay home tomorrow," she said. "I baby sit here."

"Thank you, Minna." Penny gave the broad shoulders a hug but shook her head. "We'll all be out at the airport, as planned, so you run along. And now, I *have* to dash!"

Parri was almost asleep. Her eyelashes drooped on her flushed round cheeks, and Penny only threw her one last loving look before she dashed out. She snatched up her purse and coat, found a cab, and had almost reached the theater before she remembered that neither she nor David had telephoned each other.

Josh was standing in the stage door when she ran along the alley, and he called to her, "You cut it pretty fine today, didn't you?"

She nodded. "I've an awful lot to tell you," she panted, hurrying across the stage and into her familiar corridor. "Parri cut her head."

"Much?"

"Three stitches. It's all sewed up."

"Should I go home?"

"Hunhuh."

She flung open the door and found Ma waiting with a robe and a clean towel, and snatched them both. "Tell Brooks to hold the curtain for two minutes," she said, flinging off her dress and sailing the robe after it. "I haven't time for that thing. Put my shoes on while I do my face. Josh?" She turned to find him staring at her, looking as if a stranger had usurped her dressing room, but he came over and stood behind her, where she could see him in the mirror. "Stop worrying about Parri," she ordered, when he was only worried for her, and rubbing a cream rouge on her cheeks. "She's all right."

"I know she is or you wouldn't be here."

"That's where you're wrong," she answered grimly. "The show must go on." She wriggled one foot into a mule, asked, "Is there blood on my stocking?" and squinted an eye shut. "Drat this foundation," she groaned. "It isn't smooth."

"I'll go out and alert Brooks."

The call boy wandered along the corridor with his familiar "five minutes" chant, and Josh hurried out. "What a mess," Penny fumed, and wiped off her mouth to start over.

There was no time to think of anything but her work. The play dragged for the first few minutes and she consciously speeded it along. The audience was dotted with shoppers who rustled parcels they had bought, and many of them were late. People shifted, wriggled, rattled candy boxes and programs, and were generally distracting. Penny felt it, worked hard to stop it; and it seemed a long time before she won them and held them still.

When she was back in her dressing room at the end of the long afternoon, she shut Ma out and threw herself down to rest. "I'm tired," she said to Josh, who was sitting there, waiting. "What a day. I know I ought to go home as fast as I can, but I'll simply have to relax a minute. I'm pooped."

"You don't need to go home," he answered. "I've spent the afternoon with Parri and she's fine. It's better that you don't go because she'll only hang onto you and make you dance through a hoop."

"Perhaps you're right." She leaned back and wearily closed her eyes. "Did Trudy give you the rest of the news?" she asked. "About Mums and Dad coming home?"

"I've had the works. I talked with David, and they'll be here early, the whole family. Everything's under control."

"Thank you, darling. As the comic bicycle rider used to say in vaudeville, 'Isn't this a silly way to earn a living?'"

"Um." He sat watching her as she lay among the pillows on the chaise longue. He sat until he thought she was asleep then stood up quietly and prepared to slip out, but she opened her eyes.

"Josh," she said, "I've been thinking. Come back here."

She moved ever so little so he could sit beside her; and when he was facing her, she reached for his hand and held it. "Such a lot happened today," she said. "I lost one servant for sure, and may lose the other one. I saw my child hurt, and I held her while a doctor hurt her even more—and I came through it all and subdued a fractious audience. That's pretty good—for me, isn't it?"

"It's almost a miracle," he agreed, because she wanted him to.

"But I did it. I stood right up and faced things as they came."

"Don't you always?"

"Oh, *no!*" Her eyes were wide and dark as they looked into his. "I never do," she said. "Do I?"

"I've always thought so. You may go backward to come forward, but it's always been my observation that you get there. In mighty fine fashion, too. Haven't you ever noticed it?"

"No-o," she said with troubled sincerity. "It seems to me that I muddle along, getting nowhere."

He put his hand out to stroke her hair but she suddenly flopped over and pinned it beneath her cheek. "Oh, Josh," she sighed happily, "do you think I've grown up at last?"

He hid a smile at her childish pose. Her red dress was in wads and wrinkles, her knees were drawn up almost to her chest, and half of her hung off the other side of the narrow couch. "The Lord forbid," he prayed fervently, pulling her back to safety and holding her close. "Life would be endlessly dull if you had. But let's not worry about it, darling," he added. "I don't think the time will ever come."

"All right, but I can be preparing for it." Penny loved the safe haven of his arms and rested her head against his shoulder. "I've changed my mind," she said, "about this being a silly way to earn a living. It's a lovely, *happy* way."